Once
upon
a time
in
India

To the children of the world...

Once
upon
a time
in
India

EDITED BY
NITA BERRY, DEEPA AGARWAL

DESIGN BY
ATANU ROY

ASSOCIATION OF WRITERS AND ILLUSTRATORS FOR CHILDREN

MACMILLAN

Once Upon a Time in India

(An anthology of folk tales)

These folk tales from different states of India have been retold by
the members of the Association of Writers and Illustrators for Children
(AWIC). The AWIC is the Indian Section of the International Board on Books for Young People
(IBBY). It aims to promote understanding and peace in the world through children's books. The
Indian Council for Cultural Relations, ICCR, works towards furthering and strengthening the
bonds of understanding through cultural exchanges. AWIC and ICCR cooperated to publish this
anthology of folk tales from India which brings children of the world colourful glimpses of
Indian culture, based essentially on the principle of "Vasudeva Kutumbakam" – or The World is
One Family.

© Association of Writers and Illustrators for Children (Indian BBY)
Nehru House, 4 Bahadur Shah Zafar Marg
New Delhi – 110002
Tel.: 91-11-43603831, 23316970-74
E-mail: info@awic.in
Website: www.awic.in
The first publication of this book was made possible with financial support from the Indian
Council for Cultural Relations, New Delhi

Honorary Adviser - Nilima Sinha
Editorial Board - Girija Rani Asthana, Surekha Panandiker, Nita Berry

Published in English 2018 by Macmillan
an imprint of Pan Macmillan Publishing India Private Limited
707, Kailash Building, 26 K. G. Marg, New Delhi - 110001
www.panmacmillan.co.in

Pan Macmillan, 20 New Wharf Road, London N1 9RR
Basingstoke and Oxford
Associated companies throughout the world
www.panmacmillan.com

This book was nominated for the prestigious IBBY Honour List.

ISBN: 978-93-86215-57-4

Printed at Shree Maitrey Printech Pvt. Ltd.
A-84, Sector-2, Noida (U.P.)

PREFACE

Folk stories have a timeless and universal appeal. Young and old, all succumb to the magic in the words, "Long, long ago," or, "Once upon a time," and listen, spellbound, to tales of princes and kings, sly jackals and singing donkeys, wily courtiers and beautiful nymphs.

Children everywhere love Cinderella, Snow White, Brer Rabbit and other western tales. Through this book we would like to present to them a collection of tales enjoyed by generations of children in India. Some of these much-loved stories may be poignant, others full of humour and wit, but all evoke the warmth of a childhood spent in close contact with caring elders. In fact, our rich heritage of folk tales, myths, legends and other popular children's stories needs to be recorded before it is lost to the coming generations. At the same time, the stories deserve international recognition for the value-based, wholesome entertainment that they can provide to children.

The Association of Writers and Illustrators for Children (AWIC), represents writers, illustrators, publishers and those interested in better books for children. Founded by the late Mr. Shankar Pillai, who pioneered the children's book movement in India, it has encouraged talented and creative people to write and illustrate for children. Our Indian illustrators can compare with the best anywhere in the world and many have won international renown.

AWIC is also the Indian branch of the International Board on Books for Young People (IBBY). It is amongst the foremost goals of this worldwide organisation to promote international understanding through children's books. IBBY believes that exposure to other cultures and lifestyles through interesting stories and attractive illustrations helps children understand and appreciate the diversity of nations, leading to the promotion of peace and tolerance throughout the world.

This book is a small step in the direction of such an aim. Through charming illustrations and captivating stories we present Indian tradition and culture in a splendid variety. It is not only entertaining, it is informative as well, since the stories and pictures represent the different regions of India and depict local flavours and traditions.

We owe our gratitude to Ms. Najma Heptullah, Chairperson, Indian Council for Cultural Relations, without whose inspiration and encouragement this book would never have been published. She understood the importance of targeting the young and felt that a children's book could be a good cultural ambassador. We also appreciate the fact that she recognized the potential of our authors and artists and entrusted the work to us.

We hope that the book will help promote an understanding of the culture and traditions of India and will be enjoyed by children everywhere.

Nilima Sinha
President, Association of Writers and Illustrators for Children (AWIC)
Vice-President, International Board on Books for Young People (IBBY)

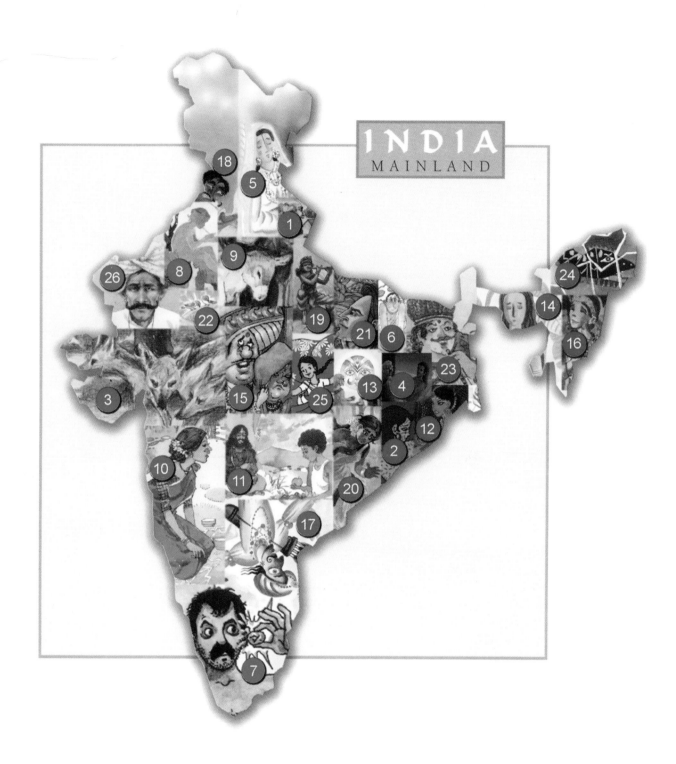

INDIA
MAINLAND

Sketch map not to scale.

To unravel this jigsaw puzzle of pictures, match the number
on the map to the story and its region on the Contents Page.

Contents

The Two Travellers

A STORY FROM HARYANA

GIRIJA RANI ASTHANA
ILLUSTRATED BY
SUJASHA DAS GUPTA

In a village in Haryana lived a farmer named Chowdhary Hari Singh. His home was on the main highway and weary travellers often knocked at his door for shelter and food. Hari Singh loved such unexpected visitors and readily offered them his hospitality. He would tell his wife, "How lucky I am that so many guests come to my house and give me a chance to serve them!"

"Yes, guests are just like God. To serve them is like serving God," she would agree.

Gradually it became such a habit with him, that at mealtimes he would wait anxiously for tired travellers to drop in. He would welcome them, offer them food and only after they had dined would he have his meal. He made it a rule not to eat unless he had hosted at least two guests.

But a day came when no one knocked at his door. Hari Singh waited and waited in vain. Soon it was dinnertime. His wife came to him and said, "Your food has gone cold. Why don't you eat now?"

"How can I? I have not fed any guests!" he objected.

"Look, this is the festival season. Diwali is just two days away, so there are very few people on the road. You can make an exception this time."

"No, I have vowed to eat only after feeding two weary travellers. I will go out and look for someone in need of food and rest."

Chowdhary Hari Singh went out. For a long time he roamed around on the highway looking out for tired wayfarers. But he couldn't find anyone.

Soon he was tired and hungry and longed to go home, but how could he return without his travellers? Seeing a sweet shop across the road, he went and sat down on a cot in front of it.

"Please, can you give me some water?" he asked the shopkeeper.

The man knew Hari Singh. He offered him sweets along with a glass of water. The sweets were actually toys made of sugar-candy for the Diwali festival and the shop was full of them, in every shape. There were birds, lions, ducks and even human figures.

"You are looking very tired, Chowdhary. What's the matter?" the shopkeeper enquired.

"Today was an unlucky day," Hari Singh replied despondently. "No one came to my house for food and rest - and you know I don't eat unless I have fed two travellers. I am really very tired and hungry."

The shopkeeper thought for some time. He looked at the sugar-candy toys in his shop. Here was his chance to make a permanent customer in Hari Singh! He picked up two dolls and brought them to Hari Singh.

"Take these dolls home and offer them food the way you would to real travellers."

"...But...how can I...I mean they are not real travellers!" Hari Singh looked puzzled.

"It's very simple. We make offerings to idols of gods and goddesses, don't we, before breaking a fast? You can do the same with these toys. After all, guests are like God for us."

As Hari Singh was very hungry the idea appealed to him. He took the sugar-candy dolls home and told his wife what the sweet seller had said.

"It's a marvellous idea!" she exclaimed. She was worried because if her husband didn't eat, neither could she, and she was now very hungry.

That day Hari Singh offered food to the two sugar-candy 'travellers' and ate his food contentedly.

The next day, when real travellers appeared, he fed them and gave the sugar-candy dolls to his eight-year old son.

The boy was delighted. "What luck!" he said happily. "I hope this happens often."

And it did happen, again and again. When no one came to Hari Singh's house, he would go to the sweet shop, buy two sugar-candy dolls, bring them home and feed them. The next time, when real travellers arrived, his son got to eat the sweets. The boy began to look forward to the days when no guests came by, so that more dolls could be bought.

Many days passed and once again no visitors came to Hari Singh's house, so he went to the sweet shop and bought his two 'travellers'. His son was happy and looked forward to eating them.

The next evening, there was a knock at the door. Hari Singh opened it to find two weary souls outside.

"Welcome!" he said, and led them into the house. Both father and son were very happy to see them - the father because he loved to welcome guests, and the son because he knew he would feast on two sugar-candy 'travellers' now.

Hari Singh offered the men water to wash their hands and feet and made them comfortable on two cots. The servant brought them two tall glasses of buttermilk and sweets.

"Please drink this while dinner is being prepared," he smiled.

After the travellers had finished eating, the servant brought in a *hukkah* for the guests to smoke.

"Do you come from far?" Hari Singh enquired with interest.

"Oh, yes, from beyond the Hindukush mountains," they replied.

"That's very interesting. Please tell me all about your travels," Hari Singh urged.

The two men had lots to tell Hari Singh. Their stories were so fascinating that Hari Singh forgot everything as he listened to them. Time flew by and soon it was dinnertime.

His son, on the other hand, was not interested in their tales at all but waited impatiently to eat the sugar-candy 'travellers'. When the boy saw no sign of the elders getting up for dinner, he went to his father and whispered loudly, "Father, can I eat one of the travellers?"

"No. Let them have their food first. Only then can you eat," Hari Singh remonstrated sternly.

Disappointed, the son left, glaring at the guests.

The men overheard what he had said and their ears pricked up.

"What does this mean? *Eat* one of the travellers?" they wondered. But they kept quiet.

After some time the boy returned and asked his father the same question.

"Oh! I have told you. Let them have their dinner first, then you can eat them both," replied Hari Singh, irritated.

The guests became really alarmed now. Why was the boy coming in and asking the same question again and again? They exchanged nervous glances.

"Is there something that we don't know?" one gestured.

"Something is not right," the other shook his head. Reluctantly, they continued to tell their stories.

As time passed, the boy became more and more impatient. He came in once more and said, "Father, either you feed them or I am going to eat the two travellers."

"Oh, be patient, son! I've told you to let them finish their meal. Once they have dined, you can eat them both," Hari Singh frowned.

The travellers were panic-stricken. Who were these people? Were they demons or evil spirits who lured innocent travellers with the promise of food and shelter, only to gobble them up?

"It seems that they will not eat us till we have had our dinner. The best way to save our lives is not to eat, come what may!" whispered one of the men into his companion's ear.

When the son entered yet again and pestered his father for the 'travellers', Hari Singh relented. He requested the guests to have dinner.

The men were waiting for this. They said firmly, "We are not hungry. We had our dinner in the last village we stopped at."

"But surely that was a long while ago. You must be hungry again. Please eat something," Hari Singh insisted.

"We are not hungry. We don't want to eat anything," the travellers replied stubbornly.

"But you must, or I will have to go hungry too. How can I eat unless my guests have eaten?" Hari Singh persisted.

Just then, the boy gave his ultimatum. "Father, either you feed them or I am going to eat the 'travellers'."

It was the last straw. Terrified, the two men jumped up. "We don't want any food. We just want to leave!" they gasped.

Hari Singh was desperate too. If the travellers left without eating, how could he have his meal? And he was really hungry now.

"You can't leave like this," he said, blocking their way.

The men looked at each other, thinking, "Just look at the way he's insisting! We are not going to become dinner for father and son!" They shook their heads firmly again.

Hari Singh continued to press them and they kept refusing. Meanwhile, his son began to throw tantrums, yelling that he was going to eat the 'travellers'.

Soon everyone was screaming and shouting. Hearing the din the neighbours became worried and rushed into the house.

"What's the matter? Why are you all shouting?" they asked in surprise.

"It's just as well that you've come, friends!" exclaimed the relieved travellers. "Please save our lives!"

"Save your lives? But from whom?" The neighbours were puzzled.

"See, this gentleman here, he invited us home for dinner...."

"And they are refusing to eat," interrupted Hari Singh.

"Because we know that once we have eaten, this boy will gobble us up...."

"What! Why would he do that?" the astonished neighbours cried.

"We overheard the father telling his son to wait till we have dined and then he could eat 'both the travellers'!"

When Hari Singh heard this, he burst out laughing. He laughed and laughed but the travellers were not amused at all.

"What's so funny? Are we telling lies?" they demanded.

With great difficulty Hari Singh controlled himself. He went inside and brought the two sugar-candy dolls. "Yes," he said. "I told my son to eat the travellers after you had eaten. These are the 'travellers' he wanted to eat!"

As everyone gazed at him, puzzled, he turned to his neighbours and said, "You know that I don't eat till I have fed two travellers. When no one comes by, I get these dolls from the sweet shop and feed them instead. I call them 'travellers'. Afterwards, when real travellers come and dine with me, my son eats the sugar-candy 'travellers'. He was waiting to eat them today too, and got impatient."

He started laughing again and one by one the neighbours joined in. The guests smiled sheepishly, and then followed Hari Singh into his house. They had a hearty meal together, and the little boy got to eat his 'travellers' finally!

The state of Haryana in the north of India has been a cradle of Indian culture and civilisation. A rendezvous for diverse races, cultures and faiths, these met, fused and crystallised into something uniquely Indian here. Hindu saints and Sikh Gurus traversed this land, spreading their message of universal love and brotherhood.

The people of Haryana are simple, straightforward, enterprising and hardworking. They have preserved their old religious and social traditions. They love to welcome guests home at any time of the day. Indeed, they consider them equal to God.

The Needle Prince

A STORY FROM BENGAL

SWAPNA DUTTA

ILLUSTRATED BY
VIKY ARYA

Once upon a time there lived a prince. His best friend was a lowly cowherd. While the prince learned how to be a king, the cowherd's time was spent tending his cows and goats. But sometimes they played together. The cowherd played on his flute and the prince listened happily.

"Will you forget me when you are king?" the cowherd would ask sometimes.

"Never!" said the prince. "I shall make you my chief adviser."

"But will you have time to listen to my flute?"

"I shall give you a flute made of gold," the prince would reply.

Years flew by. The prince and the cowherd went their different ways, as a matter of course. The prince was busy learning all that a king needs to know to rule a kingdom. The cowherd continued to care for his cattle and play on his flute. But he never made another friend.

After some time the prince, now a young man, married a beautiful princess called Kanchanmala. He completely forgot the friend of his childhood and did not even call him to his wedding. However, the cowherd went to the palace uninvited to congratulate his friend. The prince did not recognize him and threw him out of the palace. The cowherd left quietly, with tears in his eyes. But no one had the time to see how he felt.

And then a strange thing happened. When the prince woke up the next morning he found that his entire body was covered with hundreds and thousands of needles!

There were needles on his face and needles on his hands.

There were needles in his hair and needles on his feet. His entire body was a huge mass of needles!

He lay there in agony, unable to move. And people began to call him the 'needle prince'.

The king, queen and Kanchanmala were shocked to see his plight. Everyone tried to pull out the needles. But they soon realised that it was a hopeless task! The moment they pulled one needle out, another appeared in its place. So they made no headway at all.

"Oh dear! What shall we do?" cried the king and queen.

"Go and visit every place of pilgrimage until he is cured!" advised the royal priest. "Kanchanmala should stay back and try to lessen his pain."

Weeping bitterly, the king and queen left for the pilgrimage. Kanchanmala sat by the prince and pulled needles out all day long, until her hands were sore and bleeding. One morning, bruised and tired, she went to take a dip in the river, thinking it would make her feel better. She saw a young woman sitting on the bank of the river.

"Do you need a maid, fair queen?"

"I need someone to help me pull out needles. Can you do it?"

"Of course," she replied.

"Wait till I take a dip in the water," said Kanchanmala.

"The water is muddy. Let me hold your clothes and jewels," said the woman.

Not realising what the woman was up to, Kanchanmala left everything with her and plunged into the river.

Kanchanmala had barely taken a dip when she heard an arrogant voice say, "Hurry up, woman! Don't take all day. You have a lot of chores to do!"

Kanchanmala looked up amazed and found the woman dressed in her clothes and jewels.

"I am the queen now," she said, laughing. "I've tricked you properly, haven't I? No one can possibly find me out!"

Kanchanmala was a bride and she always had her face veiled, as is the custom in Bengal. So the people in the palace did not realise that the woman in Kanchanmala's clothes was an imposter. The only people who could have found the imposter out were the old king and queen. And they were away on pilgrimage. The prince was in too much pain to think about anything else.

The imposter had a marvellous time ordering everyone about and punishing people for no rhyme or reason, sending them to prison or having their heads chopped off. Everyone in the palace was shocked by the change in the queen's character. Kanchanmala had been such a gentle, soft-spoken woman. They did not suspect that it was a different person altogether! The imposter made poor Kanchanmala work all day and didn't allow her to go anywhere near the prince. It might get very awkward indeed, if Kanchanmala somehow managed to tell him the truth.

One day Kanchanmala could bear it no longer and begged permission to go and take a dip in the river. The imposter agreed because she knew that Kanchanmala would not be able to do or prove anything by herself.

Poor Kanchanmala sat on the bank of the river and cried bitterly for having fallen into an imposter's trap, from which there was no escape. Then she suddenly pricked up her ears. A man sitting under a tree nearby was singing a queer song:

"If I had a hundred needles I would buy a town,
If I had a thousand needles I would buy a crown,
If I had ten thousand needles I would dance and sing,
If I had a hundred thousand needles I would be a king!"

Kanchanmala was astonished. Who was this strange man, wanting needles, of all things?

She said, "I can give you all the needles you want but you will have to pull them out yourself. Can you?"

The man nodded. Kanchanmala burst into tears.

"Dear sister, why do you cry?" he asked.

Kanchanmala broke down at his kind words and told him the whole story.

"Don't worry. If you do all I say, everything will soon be fine. Take me to the palace with you and tell them that I am a great astrologer come from a far off land."

It was the day of *pous parvan* when the goddess Lakshmi is worshipped and special sweetmeats called *pithe* are prepared by all, both rich and poor. Women

decorate their homes with *alpana,* painting designs on the floor with rice-powder paste. All guests are made welcome. Everyone welcomed the stranger and asked him to take a seat.

"Where is the *alpana* done by the queen?" he asked, looking around. "I have come specially to see it."

"Oh, I haven't done it yet," stammered the imposter.

"Better hurry up and ask your maid to do it too. It's something every woman in the house must do. After that I must taste the *pithe* you prepare and the *pithe* prepared by your maid."

The imposter did not dare to refuse. She did not want the entire palace to see her ignoring an important tradition. So she set about it and asked Kanchanmala to get on, too. But the imposter could only prepare some crude and lumpy *aaske pithe*, which are cooked in poor households, because she did not know anything better. Kanchanmala, on the other hand, prepared many kinds of tasty, dainty *pithe* such as *khir muruli, mohan banshi, payesh* and others, always prepared in royal households. The imposter's *alpana* consisted of some crooked lines and blots. Kanchanmala's *alpana* was a thing of beauty and contained all the significant symbols of Lakshmi *puja*.

Everyone in the palace marked the difference. They were now convinced of what they had been suspecting all these days - that the new queen was an imposter.

The stranger took out a huge mass of threads from his bag and chanted,

"Needles, now your work is done,
Needles, now your cause is won!
Threads, rise up – quick at last,
And pull out every needle fast!"

The mass of threads rushed out of his hands and reached the prince smothered in needles. Every thread got into the eye of a different needle and pulled them all out at one stroke. The prince was free at last and opened his eyes to find the friend of his childhood, the cowherd, in front of him.

The prince got up and embraced him. "Oh forgive me, my friend! Forgive me for having forgotten you all these years."

"I had forgiven you long ago," said the cowherd, smiling at the prince. "But wait. My work is not yet complete." He looked at the threaded needles and said,

"Needle and thread, so tough and strong
Go, stay put where you belong!"

The needles rushed past them and stuck all over the imposter. The thread tied up her hands and feet so she was unable to run away or move. The cowherd told the prince how the imposter had tricked the queen.

"She deserves her punishment," said the people. "She will not die but will suffer like she made so many innocent people suffer, specially our queen Kanchanmala."

After that there was a grand celebration. The old king and queen returned and crowned the prince. Everyone was happy. And this time the prince did not forget his promise.

Bengal has always been particularly rich in festivals which led to the popular saying, *baro mashe tero parvan.* This literally means 'thirteen festivals in twelve months' and implies that there are many more festivals than there are months! Many festivals are special to the month of *pous*, the advent of winter. Bengal being primarily an agricultural state, some of the festivals are associated with harvesting. Two important ones are *nabanna* and *pous parvan*, celebrated as *sankrant* in other parts of India. This is observed by all - the rich and poor alike. A variety of sweets are made with the newly harvested rice, the most popular being *pithe* and *payesh*. Goddess Lakshmi is worshipped and the place is decorated with *alpana*. Certain symbols believed to be auspicious are worked into the pattern of the *alpana*.

The Wily Jackal

A STORY FROM GUJARAT

MAMATA PANDYA

ILLUSTRATED BY

NEETA GANGOPADHYA

In a river, there once lived a crocodile. One summer, all the water in the river dried up. Not a drop remained. The crocodile was in trouble because it could not live without water. As the days passed, it grew weaker and weaker in the dry river bed, close to dying.

A little distance from the river there was a water hole. There was still some water in it. But the crocodile was too weak to reach it.

A man passed by the river. The crocodile called out, "Brother, please take me where there is some water. You will be blessed if you do."

The man said, "I don't mind helping. But what if you catch me when you reach the water?"

The crocodile muttered, "*Tch, tch*, come now! How could you even think of such a thing?"

So the man picked the crocodile up, carried it to the water hole and put it inside. The crocodile began to drink water as though it had not had any for a long, long time. The man stood there and caught his breath as he watched the thirsty crocodile. Suddenly, the crocodile stretched out and grabbed the man's leg.

The man yelled out in surprise. "You promised you would not catch me. What are you doing now?"

The crocodile said, "I would not have done it, but I am so hungry. If I do not eat you, I will die of hunger. And then, your bringing me here will be all in vain." And the crocodile began to pull the man into the water.

"Wait, please wait," pleaded the man. "Let us ask someone else to decide this matter."

The crocodile thought, "Well, let me humour him for a bit. After all, I will soon be making a meal of him." So clamping harder onto the man's leg it said, "Okay. Ask then. Ask whoever you want to."

The man looked around. He saw an old cow walking by. The man called out to the cow frantically and explained the situation. Then he asked, "Now you tell me, is it right that the crocodile should eat me thus?"

The cow considered for a moment and then mooed, "Crocodile, sir, go ahead and eat this man. His whole tribe is evil. When we give them milk, they feed us

and look after us. But when we grow old and cannot give them much any more, they let us loose, and send us away. Isn't that right, man?"

The crocodile started pulling at the man harder.

"Wait, wait!" shouted the man. "Let us ask someone else."

He saw a lame horse grazing nearby. The man once again told his story to the horse. "Now tell us honestly, is this justice?"

The horse neighed in scorn. "Justice! You talk about justice, oh! man. Just look at me. My owner made me slog for so many years. Yet, as soon as my leg became lame, he put me out to pasture. Humans are all like this. Crocodile, my friend, you go ahead and eat this man."

The crocodile pulled even harder and dragged the man halfway into the water.

The man shook with fright. "Wait, wait," he stuttered. "One more time, let me ask someone. And then you may eat me if you so wish."

As he begged, a jackal slunk by. The man called out desperately, "Jackal, oh! jackal, come give us your verdict on a serious matter."

From a safe distance, the jackal called back, "What is this matter that you talk about, mister?"

Once again the man related his tale. Now the jackal was smart. It realised at once that the crocodile would not let go of the man easily. It tried a different strategy.

"I see," it said to the man, "so it is you that was stranded in the dry river bed."

"No, no!" called the crocodile. "It was I."

The jackal pretended to be confused. "I think I am all mixed up," it said. "What did you say happened next?"

The man retold that part of the story. The jackal scratched its head.

"I am sorry," it said, "my brain is working a bit slowly today. I am still very confused. Explain it again, please. What happened then?"

The crocodile was getting irritated now. "Here, let me explain. I was lying over there."

The jackal wiggled his whiskers and repeated innocently, "There, there ...where, did you say?"

Now the crocodile was really exasperated. It let go of the man's leg and climbed out from the water hole, to show that silly jackal exactly which place it had meant. The jackal quickly signalled to the man to run away. The man fled,

and so did the jackal. As it ran, the saucy jackal called out over its tail, "Ah, now I understand what you meant, crocodile. What did you say happened next?"

The crocodile realised that it had been tricked. It gnashed its teeth, and flailed its tail, and vowed that it would take its revenge on the traitorous jackal.

The rains came, and the river filled with water. The crocodile returned to live in the river. One day, it saw the jackal coming down to the river for a drink of water. The crocodile quickly dived into the mud on the riverbank and hid itself so well that only its eyes could be seen.

But the jackal was clever and alert. At the same time it could not resist teasing. Standing at a safe distance, it began to yodel,

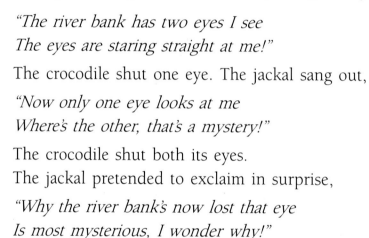

"The river bank has two eyes I see
The eyes are staring straight at me!"

The crocodile shut one eye. The jackal sang out,

"Now only one eye looks at me
Where's the other, that's a mystery!"

The crocodile shut both its eyes.
The jackal pretended to exclaim in surprise,

"Why the river bank's now lost that eye
Is most mysterious, I wonder why!"

Finally the crocodile realised that the jackal had seen it hiding in the mud. "Next time," it muttered, "you just watch it, you cheeky one."

Many days passed. The jackal was not to be seen. But one day, as it drank from the river, the crocodile swiftly swam up and grabbed the jackal's leg.

"Oh no!" thought the startled jackal. "It seems my turn has come at last." But it was crafty and it had spirit. It started to laugh aloud.

"Ha, ha, ha!" it guffawed, "Oh, you poor crocodile! Grab my leg at least; why do you hold on to that wooden post? Here's my leg, just a little to your right."

The crocodile felt foolish. What a silly mistake to have made! It quickly let go of the jackal's leg and clamped its teeth round a wooden post nearby. The jackal ran for its life. But it could not resist calling out to the crocodile, "Oh, my mistake, sir. That was indeed my leg! What you hold now is, in fact, the post!"

But now the jackal stopped coming to the river to drink water. The crocodile waited and waited. The jackal was nowhere in sight. What was to be done? Not far from the river there was a mango orchard. The jackal and its friends used to raid the orchard often, to feast on the delicious mangoes. The crocodile decided that it would go there in search of the jackal. One day it went and hid in a huge pile of fallen mangoes. Only its two eyes could be seen.

Soon the jackal arrived with its gang of friends. Right away it spotted the eyes among the mango heap. It cautioned its friends loudly, "That heap has been reserved by the government. Let's not touch it. Let's eat from the other heap."

Once again the alert jackal escaped from the jaws of the crocodile. The crocodile was really angry now, and determined to catch the jackal at any cost. It went and crept into the jackal's den, while the jackal was out.

The jackal returned home just before dawn, after a night of raiding and feasting. As it neared its den, it spotted the crocodile's eyes, glowing in the dark. Standing well outside, the jackal spoke out aloud, "How nice to see two lights glowing in my den."

The crocodile quickly shut one eye.

"Oh dear, one light seems to have gone out!" exclaimed the jackal.

The crocodile shut both eyes.

"Dear, dear," lamented the jackal in mock dismay, "the one light has gone out too. How dark it will be in my den! I don't feel like going in. Let me go to another den for now." And it quietly sneaked away to safety.

The crocodile kept a long wait in the jackal's den. But the clever jackal never came near it at all. Tired and hungry, feeling foolish and angry, the crocodile returned to the river. And it never could catch the crafty jackal!

Gujarat is a state located in the western part of India. It boasts of the country's longest coastline (for a state), with some hilly tracts, but is mostly flat and arid. Water is a precious resource, especially during the long, hot, dry summer months. It is also a land with a rich and vibrant folk culture. Its literature, music and performing arts all reflect the energy and colour of its people.

This is a favourite folk tale retold from the original Gujarati by Gijubhai Badheka, one of Gujarat's foremost educationists and storytellers. He drew upon ageless folk traditions to pen delightful tales of ordinary people and familiar animals and birds. Generations of children have grown up on these tales - told and retold by parents and grandparents.

Magic in the Mango Grove

A STORY FROM JHARKHAND

NILIMA SINHA

ILLUSTRATED BY
ATANU ROY

Long, long ago, there lived four boys in a little village at the foot of a rocky hill. They loved to swim in the stream that gurgled past the village. In the hot afternoons they played in the forest just behind their huts. When hungry, they picked the wild berries from the trees that grew there. And when evening came, making it cooler, they raced each other up the stony path to the top of the hill. Playing together, they became good friends.

Life, however, was not always play for the four boys. They had work to do as well.

One watched his father chisel wood into intricate carvings. He helped him carry logs from the forest. Together the two sawed, shaved, and carved the wood into different forms.

The second boy was a weaver's son and helped his parents weave threads into delicate fabric.

The third was the son of a goldsmith. He learnt to melt gold. Then he moulded it into jewellery delicate enough for a queen to wear.

As for the fourth, his father was a hawker who peddled his wares at the village market on Sundays. The two sold boxes of coloured powder, kohl, henna,

combs and bangles near the temple gate on Tuesdays. Village maidens flocked to buy the auspicious ware.

Time flew and soon the boys were old enough to join others on the village green. They danced through the night to the vigorous beat of drums. When the girls, flowers in their hair, sang and danced in rows they clapped heartily. Later, they drank the sweet wine made from the *mahua* flower.

But the four were not happy. One night, after work, they talked it over.

"I wish life were more exciting! I am tired of carving out the same old shapes for the same old folk," complained the wood-carver.

"You are right. It is so dull here. Our people are content with coarse homespun. I must meet others to inspire me to create finer cloth," sighed the weaver.

The goldsmith added his bit. "I can design the most fabulous of ornaments. But who will buy them here? Only the rich and aristocratic can appreciate what I make."

"I am tired of selling powders and bangles! I just wish I could be a rich trader dealing in fancy merchandise!" muttered the fourth glumly.

The four friends decided to leave the village to see the world. One morning, before the sun could peek out from behind the hill, they gathered up their tools and stole away.

With a spring in their steps and a song in their hearts they walked on. Thatched roofs and mud-smeared walls were left far behind. The hill was soon lost to sight. By evening there were no signs

of any familiar landmarks. And by the time the stars shone out, they were in the midst of lonely fields stretching far as the eye could see.

Within no time the fields had become dark. Now fear slowed their steps down. They had to find shelter somewhere.

What a relief it was when they reached a mango grove! They decided to spend the night there under a large, shady tree.

"We must keep guard. I cannot afford to lose my knives and tools," said the wood-carver.

"My spools and threads are my lifeline," added the weaver. "I must keep them safe."

"Any thief would be only too happy to steal the precious stuff that I have," said the goldsmith, clutching his bag close.

"My powders and bangles may not be as valuable as your gold. But I depend on them for my living," muttered the hawker.

"One of us must remain awake to allow the others a sound sleep," suggested the wood-carver.

"Yes, let us take turns to keep guard," the other three agreed readily.

They drew lots and it fell upon the wood-carver to keep the first watch. He tried to stay awake while the other three snored. But he felt lonely and fearful and imagined all the worst that could happen. Behind every bush monsters seemed to lurk. Each small sound reminded him of ghosts, spirits and witches. Tigers and hyenas seemed to leer at him and he imagined the greedy eyes of bandits and thieves fixed on him. At every gust of wind, every flutter of a leaf, or twitch of a twig he jumped up, alarmed.

At last the wood-carver had a brilliant idea. He dragged a log that lay under the tree close to him. As the moon swept the shadows away he began to shape the log into a statue. He was no longer afraid. The imaginary monsters, ghouls, beasts and thieves vanished. He cut, chiselled and polished the wood. Before long, he had carved out a graceful female figure. He placed it near the tree trunk, a lovely girl with the most perfect of shapes!

Finally exhausted, he woke his friend the weaver, and fell into a dreamless sleep.

The weaver's eyes fell on the figure under the tree. Was the moon playing tricks on him? What was this girl doing here? Was she a witch perhaps? He dared to draw near, and realised it was nothing but a wooden statue. It was a

beautiful figure but it had no clothes. Quickly he took out his threads and loom.

Deft fingers pulled and weaved. Silken strands flashed in and out in a rainbow of colours. Soon a beautiful fabric - soft, delicate, lay on the ground, shimmering in the moonlight. With loving hands the man wrapped the sari around the girl. Then he woke up the third friend.

Who was that charming damsel? wondered the goldsmith when he saw the wooden figure. Then he laughed aloud. What a fool he was! He had thought he had a companion for the night! But, there were no regrets. It would be a challenge to design ornaments for this lovely figure. And, it was sure to keep slumber at bay.

Soon a pile of jewellery glittered at his feet. The goldsmith strung the ornaments around the girl's neck, feet, fingers and wrists. Then he stepped back to admire his handiwork. Yes, he had done a good job.

The vendor, in turn, was awestruck at the beauty of the wooden statue. His friends had crafted a perfect shape. Yet, there was surely something missing. He dug his hands into his bag and drew out a small silver box. Inside it was a powder in a bright vermilion shade. The young man took a pinch and smeared it on the girl's forehead.

It was as if the powder had performed a magic trick! First, the figure seemed to tremble. Then the lips parted to give a gentle sigh. A deep rose blush spread over the cheeks and a delicate, lingering fragrance scented the air. The next moment, the eyelids had fluttered open. Big black eyes met the startled gaze of the young man.

The wooden statue had begun to breathe!

Amazed, the youth stepped back. "Wh…what? Wh…o?" he stammered.

The damsel cast her eyes demurely down. She raised a hand and adjusted the sari around her slender shoulders. The young man's heart missed a beat.

By now the sun was a golden disc above the horizon. One by one the others opened their eyes. Their mouths fell open as they beheld the living figure. Was it a miracle or magic? Was she real or an illusion? They tried to touch the girl who drew back in alarm. Finally, the friends found their voices.

"Isn't she beautiful?" cried the wood-carver. "To think that I made her! She is my creation." And he stepped forward to stroke a shapely arm.

"No, no, don't you dare touch her! She is mine. You left her unclothed. I gave her grace by wrapping her in a sari I wove for her! Look how intricate its weave

is!" said the weaver, pulling at the garment.

"But it is I who adorned her in priceless jewellery. See how much gold I invested in those ornaments?" said the goldsmith, pointing out his handiwork. "Each of those pieces costs a fortune. See this ring? She must be mine!"

The vendor gazed at the girl's face with tender eyes. "Let us ask her. Whom will she marry?" he gently asked.

"Me!" shouted the wood-carver. "She would not be here, had I not carved her out of a log of wood!"

"No, no, me! I gave her clothes and turned her into a lady!" insisted the weaver.

"But I invested the most in her!" protested the goldsmith.

"What is your wish?" the vendor once again turned to the girl. His voice was anxious yet hopeful.

She raised her head to look at him but did not answer.

The four friends argued heatedly and even came to blows. At last the fourth restrained the others. "Let us ask some wise person. Perhaps he will tell us what is best for the girl," he suggested, stealing another glance at the blushing maiden.

All four agreed and swore to abide by the advice. As the sun rose higher and it turned hotter, passers-by came to rest in the shade. Among them was a sage with a white beard. As soon as they saw him, the friends rushed to him for advice.

The sage looked long at their faces. He studied the girl. At last he gave his verdict.

"He who created the girl out of a piece of wood is her father. The one who protected her by providing garments is an elder brother. The one who gifted the ornaments is an uncle. And the person who breathed life into an inanimate beauty, and showed concern for her wishes is her husband."

The words of the wise man were so convincing that the friends had to agree.

The youth who brought her to life by putting vermilion on her forehead got to marry the damsel.

This story is narrated among the tribal people of the Chhotanagpur plateau, which spreads across the newly formed states of Jharkhand and Chhatisgarh as well as Orissa and Bengal. A picturesque region of hills, valleys and lakes, it is densely forested with trees like the flame of the forest, the *sal*, and the *mahua*. Elephants, tigers and leopards still roam in the wildlife sanctuaries. Pretty villages, with huts whose mud-smeared walls are decorated with paintings of animals and flowers, nestle near ponds and streams.

The custom in which the groom puts vermilion powder on the forehead and parting of the hair of the bride is an important part of wedding rites everywhere in north India, and is considered a proof of marriage. In fact, even now married women in many parts of the country wear vermilion in the parting of their hair.

Phyunli-
the Evening Primrose

A STORY FROM UTTARANCHAL

DEEPA AGARWAL

ILLUSTRATED BY

SUDDHASATTWA BASU

I n the forests of Uttaranchal, along the winding paths that crisscross the hillsides, or on the sides of the terraced fields, a pretty yellow flower is often seen. Unlike most flowers it blooms in the evening, perfuming the air with a delicate fragrance.

The hill people call this flower 'phyunli', though elsewhere it is known as the evening primrose.

Once, they say, there was a forest, dense with oak and rhododendron trees. In the middle of this forest was a lake, and a beautiful forest nymph named Phyunli lived near it. Her cheeks were as rosy as the first flush of dawn and her eyes the colour of the clear waters of the lake.

Phyunli lived alone in the forest. But she was not alone because the birds and animals were her family and took care of her. The parrots and thrushes fetched her the choicest wild cherries and peaches. The bears brought honey and dug up wild radishes and other edible roots for her to eat and the mischievous monkeys broke wild figs and walnuts from the trees for her.

Phyunli led a carefree life, racing the deer, swimming in the lake, or stringing garlands of wild flowers to put around her neck. At night she slept in a cave, on a bed of spongy moss and fresh green leaves.

One day, as she sat by the lake, watching a herd of deer grazing, she heard the sound of thundering hoofs. Startled, the deer sprang up and dashed away. Phyunli rose to her feet in alarm. Suddenly, an arrow whizzed through the air, just missing one of the fleeing deer. As Phyunli shrieked, a horse burst through the trees. The rider, a richly dressed young man, was fitting another arrow to his bow.

"Stop!" Phyunli cried. "Who are you? Why do you want to hurt the deer?"

The horseman came to a halt. He jumped off his horse and gazed at Phyunli, wonderstruck. He was tall and handsome, with glistening black locks and a curling moustache and his skin was as white as the snow on the mountains above.

"I'm the prince of this land," he replied. "And this forest is part of my kingdom. Who are you girl, that you stop me from hunting here?"

"I am Phyunli," the nymph replied. "I live in this forest and the birds and animals are my brothers and sisters. Please don't harm them."

The prince smiled. "Hunting is my favourite sport," he said. "But I cannot refuse a girl as lovely as you."

Phyunli smiled back. "It's good of you to listen to my request," she said. "Please sit down and rest awhile."

The prince sat down on a flat rock and Phyunli brought him water in a leaf-cup.

He accepted it gratefully, then said with a curious look, "How is it that a lovely young girl like you lives all alone in the forest? Aren't you afraid of the dangerous beasts that abound here?"

"I have always lived here," Phyunli said. "And the beasts you call dangerous are my family."

The prince shook his head, amazed. "Are you a real girl or a fairy?" he asked.

"I am...just Phyunli," the nymph replied.

Suddenly a sound filled the air - the fluttering of little wings. The birds were bringing Phyunli's evening meal. The prince watched open-mouthed as they laid a feast before her and flew away.

"You must be hungry," Phyunli said. "Please taste our humble offerings."

The prince picked up a wild fig. He had never eaten anything so delicious in his life and soon he had finished all the fruit.

But the sun was beginning to sink. The prince looked up at the reddening sky and said, "It's growing dark. I may not be able to find my way home. Can I spend the night here?"

"You are most welcome," Phyunli said.

She prepared a bed of moss and leaves for the prince beneath a shady tree and retired to her cave.

The first rays of the sun awoke the prince. He sat up, surprised to find himself in the forest. Then he remembered Phyunli. But she was nowhere to be seen. Wondering if it had all been a dream, the prince walked to the lake. As he bent to splash his face with water, he heard a footstep behind him. It was Phyunli, bringing him breakfast.

"Ah, it's you. You are real!" the prince exclaimed. "I was beginning to think I was dreaming."

Phyunli said, "It might seem like that when you return to your palace."

She fell silent as the prince ate, so he remarked, "You look troubled, Phyunli. What's the matter?"

Phyunli said hesitantly, "Prince, I wish to ask you a favour."

"What is it?" asked the prince. "If it is in my power, I will surely grant it."

"It is," Phyunli replied. "I want you to promise that you will never try to kill my brothers and sisters again."

The prince said, "Hunting is the sport of kings. But I cannot refuse you. However...you will have to promise me something too."

"What can a simple forest dweller do for a powerful prince?" Phyunli asked, puzzled.

"You can marry me," said the prince.

Phyunli gazed at him, stunned. "A forest dweller in a palace?" she said. "I belong in these woods, prince."

"Don't break my heart, Phyunli!" exclaimed the prince. "I will not be able to live without you. Please, come with me!"

He pleaded so much that Phyunli's heart melted.

"All right," she said. "But remember your promise."

She bid a tearful goodbye to the birds and the animals and mounted the prince's horse.

They had barely arrived in the city when news spread that the prince had returned from the forest with a strange girl. His parents hurried out to receive him and curious courtiers gathered around to watch.

"Thank the gods you are back safe, my son!" the king exclaimed, embracing him. "Your companions said that they lost you in the forest."

"I had a very comfortable stay there, thanks to Phyunli," replied the prince, bringing her forward. "Dear parents, with your permission, I wish to make her my wife."

The king and queen loved their son dearly, so they said, "If it makes you happy, how can we refuse you?"

There was a grand wedding. For some time Phyunli was very happy, living with the prince. She had never enjoyed such luxury before - soft beds, delicious food, beautiful clothes and jewels to wear and servants to attend to her needs. The prince was a loving husband and there was nothing in the world that she did not possess.

But as time went by, the grand walls of the palace began to close in on Phyunli. The din of the city gave her a headache. Her richly embroidered velvet *ghaghra* and silken veil weighed her down, as did her ornaments of gold and precious stones. The servants and courtiers were deceitful and scheming and often the prince was too busy to spend time with her.

Phyunli began to long for the open woods, the music of the mountain streams

and the affection of her brothers and sisters. But since she loved the prince she kept these thoughts to herself.

One day, the prince's old companions came by, saying, "It's wonderful weather for hunting. Shall we set off for the forest, your highness?"

The prince paused for a moment, and then replied, "I promised Phyunli that I would never hunt again. She says the birds and beasts are her brothers and sisters."

"You don't have to hunt," said his friends. "Just come with us for company."

The prince did not wish to hurt his friends by refusing them. "All right," he agreed. However, in his hurry to be off, he forgot to tell Phyunli.

When evening came, and the prince did not return, Phyunli asked her maids about him.

"Didn't he tell you, your highness?" they said. "He's gone hunting with his friends. They'll be away for a few days."

"Hunting!" Phyunli cried, paling. She fell into a dead faint.

The court physician was called immediately, and he managed to revive her somehow. The queen comforted her, saying, "Don't worry, my dear. He'll be back soon. He needs to spend time with his friends too."

But all Phyunli could think of was that the prince had broken his promise. She would not eat or drink and grew weaker and weaker day by day. Her rosy cheeks faded to a sickly yellow and all the medicines the physicians gave her could not restore her.

The king and queen were in despair, when the sound of hoofs was heard in the palace courtyard. The prince was back.

When he heard about Phyunli's condition, he rushed to her side. Horrified to see what had become of her, he cried, "Please forgive me for not telling you, my beloved! But I did not break my promise."

Phyunli smiled faintly and whispered, "I believe you, but it's too late now. Please take me back to the forest. And bury me where I can be near my beloved brothers and sisters always."

The prince wept bitterly but Phyunli was already drawing her last breath. He put her in a palanquin and carried her to the forest. The birds and animals wept too, as he buried her on the top of a hill, even as the last yellow rays of the sun touched it.

When winter passed and the trees began to sprout fresh leaves, a small green shoot pushed its way up from Phyunli's grave. And when the summer sun grew warmer, a pretty yellow flower was seen blooming on the hillside. The hill people named this flower 'phyunli' in memory of the girl who loved the forest and its inhabitants so dearly.

The hill state of Uttaranchal lies below the Himalaya mountains and abounds in natural beauty. Snow covered peaks and glaciers which give birth to important Indian rivers like the Ganga and Jamuna, rise above the forests of oak, rhododendron, deodar and pine which line its hillsides. Limpid lakes, waterfalls and sparkling streams add to the charm of the landscape along with valleys and meadows covered with wild flowers which bloom in different seasons. It is also a land of temples and the famous shrines of Badrinath and Kedarnath are frequented by many pilgrims.

The people of Uttaranchal have a close relationship with their surroundings, and many folk tales explaining the birth of birds and flowers exist. The story of Phyunli is one of these.

The Miracle

A STORY FROM BIHAR

THANGAM KRISHNAN

ILLUSTRATED BY
VANDANA BIST

Kesariya and his wife Kusuma were seated on a string cot in the courtyard of their house, eating their food.

"Caw!" called a crow from the mango tree in the courtyard. The aroma of food had brought it there.

"Sh-ooo!" Kusuma chased it away, holding a piece of *roti* in her hand. It fell on the ground and the crow quickly picked it up.

"There!" Kesariya exclaimed with annoyance. "This is exactly what I mean when I say that you waste my hard-earned money."

"But…it was only a small piece," protested Kusuma.

But that was Kesariya. He was so miserly that even chasing a crow with a morsel of food in one's hand was being a spendthrift.

Kusuma was fed up. Kesariya always criticised her for wasting money when he hardly gave her any. The roof of the house kept leaking during the rains and Kesariya would not repair it.

"Keep buckets under the holes. That will do," he would say.

Saving money and hoarding it gave him great pleasure. Not that Kusuma was a spendthrift, but she felt upset when even essentials were denied to her.

"I like to keep the house neat and clean, the children to eat well and to have good relations with our neighbours. What is wrong with that?" she would ask.

"It is I who work hard to make a living and hence I will do as I please." Kesariya was very particular to rub in the fact that the money was earned by him. If he wanted to save it, so should it be.

One day, Kesariya told his wife, "Kusuma, I am going to the next village. Close the door and be careful. I will return in the evening."

"What about food for you? Shall I pack some *rotis?*"

"No, no, that's not necessary," answered Kesariya. "I will manage."

It was not that Kesariya did not love his wife and children. It was only that he loved money more. "She will understand some day," he thought, as he walked towards the next village.

Kusuma too loved her husband, but she thought that money hoarded had no value - just as money wasted had none. "Some day he will understand," she sighed.

Kesariya was very tired by the time he reached the village. He went about his work, collected the money due to him and reached a sweet shop where hot *jalebis, laddus* and *puris* were being cooked. The aroma of the food, especially the hot, round, puffed up *puris* with potato curry and sweets was so inviting that he stood in front of the shop inhaling it for half an hour or so. Though he was very hungry, he was reluctant to spend any money.

"I shall have some water and go back home and eat," he told himself.

"Give me a glass of water, please," he said to the shopkeeper.

The shopkeeper gave him the water and said, "That will be five rupees."

"What! A glass of water for five rupees!" exclaimed the shocked Kesariya.

"No, the water is free. But, for enjoying the aroma of my sweets for half an hour, you will have to pay five rupees." The voice of the shopkeeper was acquiring a threatening note.

"But I did not eat anything!" protested Kesariya.

"If you had eaten, you would have had to pay ten rupees. Five rupees is the payment for inhaling the fragrance of my sweets."

Kesariya thought for some time. "I see…All along I had thought I was smarter than others at making and saving money, but this man seems to be a master. No, I will not let him get the better of me."

He took five rupees in coins, put them in his pocket and jingled them loudly.

"Listen carefully," he told the bewildered shopkeeper, jingling his coins once again, "that was your five rupees."

"What do you mean?" asked the angry shopkeeper.

"As payment for enjoying five rupees' worth of the aroma of your food, you have listened to the sound of coins amounting to five rupees. We are now quits."

The shopkeeper was taken aback, but he quietly accepted Kesariya's explanation. "I thought I was the ace miser around here, but this man is one better!" he said to himself.

Kesariya too secretly admired the shopkeeper. "Ah! What a miser," he thought. "I am glad I could learn something from him."

Kesariya had a new vigour in his step as he walked home, humming a tune. "I must tell this to Kusuma. She cannot complain about me any more."

Kusuma was indeed glad to see him and served him his food. Kesariya narrated the day's incident and said admiringly, "Ah! What intelligence! He is a genius. He must be a master in the art of saving money! But I was no less." He looked up for appreciation.

Kusuma was disappointed. Of all the people in the world, he had to meet another miser, even though he had gone so far away from home! She felt hopelessly discouraged. How will Kesariya ever change, she wondered?

The next morning, when he got up, Kesariya's one thought was the hot, puffed-up *puris*. He longed to have some right away.

"Kusuma," he said peremptorily, "make me some *puris* and spicy potato curry to go with them. I'm longing to eat some."

"Wait for some time," she replied patiently. "I'll make some *puris* for the entire family. The children would like to have some too when they return from school, and I will give a few to the neighbours."

"Are you crazy? Why bring the children into this? They must have had their meal," protested Kesariya. "There is no need to overfeed them."

By this time Kusuma's interest in making the *puris* was dwindling.

"And as for the neighbours…" added Kesariya scornfully, "as if we are rajas or maharajas!"

"Then I will make just enough for the two of us."

"Why? You did not feel like eating *puris*. It is only I who wanted them. Moreover, there's no point in wasting so much oil. Make *puris* just for me."

Shaking her head, Kusuma went about her work. "Only a miracle will change him," she thought wistfully, "and miracles do not happen easily."

She boiled some potatoes and prepared the curry first. Appetising smells came floating into the room where Kesariya was sitting. Soon Kusuma started frying the *puris* in *ghee*. The odour was so tempting that Kesariya had to praise his wife's culinary skills.

"But wait, let me close the doors and windows. Otherwise, the neighbours will get wind of it and come over to find out what's cooking…and then we may have to offer them some too."

Kesariya went quickly to close the door. But what did he see? There, in front of the house, stood a holy man holding a begging bowl.

Kusuma could not bear to refuse him. "Let me give him one *puri* at least," she pleaded.

"All right," Kesariya said grudgingly. "Give him the smallest."

But as soon as Kusuma touched the smallest *puri* in the basket, it turned into the biggest. She touched another and that too became the biggest. This went on for some time. She gazed at her husband, bewildered.

Kesariya got impatient and told Kusuma to hurry and feed the holy man so that he might get rid of him and have his own lunch. Kusuma was very happy.

This was the first time that she was feeding a *sadhu* in her house.

She offered him a seat and served the *puris* with the potato curry in a sparkling clean plate. But, even as he ate, each *puri* he took was replaced by another in the basket.

After eating, the holy man drank the cold water that Kusuma offered him from the earthenware pot and blessed them both.

"Anything else that we can do, *swamiji?* " Kusuma asked politely.

"Yes, daughter, if you do not mind, there are a few others who have travelled with me and are staying on the outskirts of this village. They must be hungry as well. Can you feed them too?"

"Why not?" Saying this, Kusuma picked up the basket of *puris* and the pot of curry and turned to Kesariya. "Lock the door and come with me," she said. She had suddenly become very bold.

Kesariya did not like all this one bit. But, in front of the holy man, he could not say anything. Contrary to his nature, he was tongue-tied.

When they reached the place, they found hundreds of *sadhus* waiting. Kusuma and Kesariya started serving them one by one. To their surprise, as they were served, the *puris* in the basket were replaced by others. And even after all of them had eaten, the basket was still full of hot *puris* and the vegetable pot brimmed with curry.

The holy man blessed the couple. "As long as you share your food, this basket will never be empty."

When the two returned home, they shared the *puris* with their neighbours and servants. And when the children came back from school, they all sat down and ate together as a family. Kesariya had never been so happy and neither had Kusuma.

After all, the miracle *had* happened!

This story is originally from the state of Bihar which is situated in the northern part of India and is famous for its rich, ancient culture. The rustic people of Bihar are simple and down-to-earth. While projecting a picture of docility, its women can also take their own decisions when the occasion demands, as Kusuma does in this story. As in other parts of India, the people of Bihar respect holy and learned people.

The Challenge

A STORY FROM TAMIL NADU

DEVIKA RANGACHARI

ILLUSTRATED BY
TAPAS GUHA

Long ago in Tamil Nadu, in the south of India, there lived a king who had a very able minister. The king trusted the minister completely and the minister, in turn, was devoted to his king.

On one occasion, the king remarked, "I have plans for making this kingdom the strongest in the land. After all, man can achieve anything by his efforts."

"We must wait for the right time, Sire," the minister said. "Yes, man's efforts and will are important but if the time is not right, nothing can be achieved."

"No, no!" the king declared. "You are wrong."

"No, Sire," persisted the minister. "If the time is not favourable, man's efforts will be worthless."

The king paced the floor impatiently. "We will see who is right," he said.

Just then his gaze alighted on a poor man who was passing by. His clothes were torn and black with dirt, and his body was thin and frail. The king summoned the wretched creature and asked him what he did for a living.

"I sell thread," replied the poor man, his eyes wide with fear and his breath coming in frightened gasps.

The king turned to his minister with a triumphant air. "I will make this man rich in one month."

He turned to the poor man. "Don't be afraid," he said. "I want to help you with your business. Take these gold coins and use them well. By your efforts, you will have good sales and become wealthy before long."

"He cannot become rich with this money alone," the minister objected. "The time must be favourable too."

The king did not reply and they watched the poor man depart, a grateful smile on his face.

After going some distance, the poor man stopped to count the coins. Then he extracted a few coins from the bundle. Thereafter, he tore a piece of cloth from his garments and tied the rest of the coins in it, placing the bundle on his head. He then bought a banana and began to peel it.

All of a sudden, he heard a whirring sound and a rush of air

grazed his cheek. A huge eagle flew into his face, trying to wrest the banana from his grip. The poor man screamed and threw up his hand to shield his face while holding the fruit out of the bird's grasp. The eagle then seized the bundle on the man's head in its beak and was gone in an instant. The poor man walked home slowly, tears of disappointment gushing from his eyes.

In a few days' time, the king visited the poor man to find how he had used the money. He listened to the story in shocked silence.

"Who could have known this would happen?" he remarked. "Do not despair, however. I will give you some more gold coins, but be careful with the money this time. Use it well. You will be rich before long."

Meanwhile, the poor man thought long and hard and finally decided to keep the money in an old pitcher that contained husk.

"It should be safe here," he said to himself. "But I will not let my wife know in case she tells someone."

The following day while the poor man was away, his wife decided to clear all the clutter away from the hut. When her gaze fell on the pitcher full of husk, she decided to dispose of it at once. As luck would have it, a husk merchant was passing by and she hailed him.

"Do you want to buy some husk?" she asked.

"Yes," said the merchant. "But I do not have any vessel to carry it in."

The poor man's wife was struck with an idea. Why not sell the pitcher along with the husk? After all, it was old and cracked and they could use the extra money.

And so, the man paid for the pitcher and husk and, thereafter, took it to the market to sell. However, he could not find a buyer as the husk was very old. Accordingly, he kept the pitcher in a corner of his house, meaning to sell it as soon as he could.

Meanwhile, when the poor man returned, his wife showed him the money and waited to be praised for her cleverness. Instead, he wrung his hands in despair and told her what she had done.

"We have lost the gold coins due to your foolishness!" he shouted.

"It is your fault as well," retorted the wife, torn between anger and regret. "Why didn't you tell me where you'd hidden the money?"

"What is the use of arguing now when the money's gone?" responded the poor man dully.

In a month's time, the king set out with his minister to visit the poor man again. As before, when he heard the tale, the king was incredulous.

"How could this be?" he demanded.

The minister, meanwhile, picked up a nail and held it out to the poor man.

"Take this," he said. "If the time is right, you can become a rich man with the help of this nail."

The poor man took it from the minister's hand, not daring to do otherwise. However, as soon as his grand visitors had left, he let the nail drop to the floor and thought no more about it.

Late that night, a fisherman knocked at his door.

"Forgive me for disturbing you at this hour," he said, "but I am desperate. I need to use my net tomorrow but one nail is missing from it. The market is closed so I have asked all my neighbours, but I cannot find the right size of nail anywhere. Can you help me?"

The poor man was about to shake his head when he remembered the nail that the minister had given him. He instructed his little boy to hunt for it on the floor and when it was located, at long last, in a dark corner, he held it out to the fisherman.

The fisherman uttered a cry of relief. "This is just the right size!" he cried. "How much do I give you for it?"

"Nothing," replied the poor man. "I have no use for this nail."

"But I must give you something!" insisted the grateful fisherman. "As you have helped me at the right time, I will give you the first fish that I catch in my net tomorrow morning."

He was back, the following day, with an enormous fish in his hands. "This is the first one I caught," he said.

The poor man thanked the fisherman and gave the fish to his wife to cook. He watched her idly as she cut the fish in two and then a cry of surprise escaped his lips. His wife shouted out in wonder too for there, nestling in the belly of the fish, was a huge diamond.

The poor man seized the gem with trembling hands, his delighted eyes reflecting its sparkle.

"Our worries are over!" he declared. "We will never be poor again."

In no time at all, the poor man sold the diamond to a jeweller for a huge sum of money. He spent some of it in building a big house over the ruins of his hut and invested the rest in establishing a business.

And so, when the king and his minister came by in a month's time, they were pleasantly surprised to see the signs of his prosperity. The poor man (who, of

course, was poor no more) came running out and fell at their feet.

"I owe all this to you, kind sires!" he cried. "How can I ever repay you?"

When he narrated the story, the king's face shone with pleasure and he asked, "How did you sell the diamond and set up the business?"

The poor man replied, "Sire, I wanted to invest the treasure as soon as I could, so I went to the jeweller at once. He had gone to his brother's house, so I waited for him to return. Within a few hours, I had sold the gem. Then I ran to the market to buy the place for my shop. I hired some apprentices and had the shop ready within a few days. Meanwhile, I saw to the construction of this new house, to the hiring of the servants, to the buying of cloth and other general affairs."

"Sire," said his wife proudly, "he was so busy that he did not have time even for his meals. But now, at long last, we are able to enjoy our wealth."

The poor man broke in eagerly, "Please do us the honour of dining with us today, sires," he pleaded.

"We surely will," smiled the king.

As the day was fine, they sat out in the garden while the servants prepared the meal. The poor man's small son was flying his kite and stealing looks at the grand visitors, hoping they would notice his skills.

Shortly after, the king's coachman appeared. "Sire, the bullocks are very hungry," he said. "I need to give them some husk."

The king turned to the poor man. "Do you have any husk for them?" he asked.

"No, Sire," replied the poor man. "But I will send a servant to get some from the market."

As he gave the order to his servants, his little son tugged at his clothes.

"My kite is stuck in that tree, father," he murmured. "What will I do now?"

The poor man sent a servant to climb the tree and rescue the kite. This was no mean task, for the tree was tall with a smooth bark and the kite was stuck fast to one of the gnarled branches. However, the servant persevered and returned, trying to disentangle a dirty cloth from the kite.

"Give it to me," said the poor man and, as he took hold of the cloth, a shower of gold coins fell out of it.

"Oh!" he cried, amazed. "This is the bundle that the eagle snatched from me!"

While they exclaimed delightedly at this turn of events, the servant returned from the market with a pitcher full of husk.

"This was the only pot of husk I could find, Sire," he gasped, his face beaded with sweat. "None of the husk merchants had enough to feed the bullocks and finally I found this tucked away in a shop quite some distance from the market."

The poor man took one look at it and said dazedly, "This is my old pitcher! I recognize it by the crack across its mouth." A moment later, he had recovered the gold coins that still lay buried in the husk.

The minister turned to the king with a triumphant air. "Sire, was I not right?" he exclaimed. "You agree now that time is all important?"

To his surprise, the king shook his head. "No, my friend," he said. "Man's efforts are equally important and I will show you how. Had we not made the effort to make this man rich, he would never have become so. Had he not made efforts to secure his wealth, he would not have lost it. Had the little boy not taken the effort to find the nail, they would never have got the fish with the diamond. Had the man not made efforts to immediately invest his wealth, he would not have such a good business or such a beautiful house. Had the servant not climbed the tree with so much effort, the bundle would never have been found. And had the other servant not made the effort to scour the market for husk, the pitcher would never have been found. This man is rich not just because the time is lucky for him but because he took the challenge to make honest efforts to this end."

The minister immediately realised the truth of this statement.

Even today, it is believed that while good times and bad times come to all, man can move mountains if he so desires.

Tamil Nadu is located in south India. The home of the Tamils, it has a glorious past and vibrant culture. Tamil Nadu has witnessed the rule of great dynasties like the Pallavas and the Cholas. The region spans varying physical divisions like mountains, forests, arid areas, fertile plains and coastal regions and the people are simple and deeply religious. Rice is their staple diet and their economy is based largely on agriculture.

The state is famed for its magnificent temples and rich traditions in music, dance, arts and crafts. Tamil Nadu is also noted for its folklore that has passed on from generation to generation through an equally strong tradition of storytelling.

The Singing Spirit

A STORY FROM PUNJAB

NITA BERRY

ILLUSTRATED BY

JAGDISH JOSHI

There was enchantment in the air when the little shepherd played his bamboo flute. As its lilting melody wafted softly over the pathless plains of the Punjab, beasts stopped in their tracks and birds listened in wonder.

He played all day as he ran barefooted among the briars, watching his flock of sheep. His music filled his lonely hours with its sad sweetness. What is more, his sheep never strayed far and grew fat on the greens.

The little shepherd had lived with his aunt ever since his parents had died many years ago. He tried his hardest to please her, but she was always cross with him.

"Lazybones!" she would scold. "You loiter all day long and do not watch the sheep. One day they will stray far away and be eaten by wolves! And then how will we earn a living?"

One day she was angrier than usual. "Lazybones! Let me throw that useless flute of yours away. It makes you idler than ever…Now off you go!" And flinging his small flute far away, she sent him to tend the flock, as always, with just two dry *rotis* to eat from morning to evening.

As it happened, the same day a great big wolf strayed into the wilds. He had a hungry gleam in his eyes. They lit up when he saw the little shepherd leading his flock. He bowed low as he came up to him and said, "Little shepherd, I have come a long, long way from yonder hills and I am very hungry. Tell me, whom shall I eat - you or your sheep?"

The little shepherd folded his hands and bowed politely. "Oh, Wolf *sahib,* I cannot tell you right now. I will have to ask my aunt when I go home. I will let you know tomorrow for sure."

"Very well," said the wolf gruffly. "Don't forget. I will be waiting for you here."

When the little shepherd brought the flock home that evening, he told his aunt about the hungry wolf's strange request.

She took one look at him and another at the fat sheep. "Well, what is there to think about? He must eat *you*, of course!" she snapped, turning away with a crooked smile.

"Very well, aunt, I will tell him tomorrow," replied the little boy without blinking.

The big wolf was waiting impatiently the next morning when the little shepherd led his flock out onto the grassy plain. He went up to the wolf and bowed, "Wolf *sahib,* my aunt has said that you may eat me."

Even the wolf felt sorry for the little shepherd whom he would soon eat. "Is there anything I can do for you, lad, after I have eaten you up?" he asked kindly.

The little shepherd nodded. "After you have eaten me up, I would like you to string my anklebone and hang it from the tree that overlooks the pond yonder."

And so it was done. The wolf ate the little shepherd boy and hung his anklebone just as he had asked. There it dangled from the tree in the sunlight and danced with the breeze.

Now it so happened that one dark night three robbers passed that way. They were laden with treasures stolen from the king's palace. They sat under the drooping tree by the pond to divide their booty. Dishes of gold and precious stones were spread all around. Suddenly a jackal howled and the robbers almost jumped out of their skins in fright. It was a bad omen. Just then the thread from which the anklebone dangled snapped - and fell on the head of their leader.

With a cry he was on his feet. "Run! Run! We are being attacked!" he shouted frantically to his companions. The robbers fled for their lives, leaving their booty behind by the pond.

"Aha! Now I shall be rich!" a little voice tinkled from the shadows. "I won't have to work for a living anymore. I can feed my thirsty friends and play my flute all day!"

Before the sun arose the next morning, a sweet and haunting melody had filled the air. The notes were unmistakable. As they wafted over the endless plains, the deer pricked up their ears, cattle lowed and the birds twittered in wonder. Was it possible? Could it be true? Was their beloved little shepherd back amidst them?

Then a joyful song echoed softly through the wilds -

> *"Grieve no more, loving friends,*
> *I came to no harm!*
> *Your little shepherd boy*
> *Is now Gitta Ram!"*

There was magic in the air once again! The birds and the beasts gathered around the little figure by the pond, who played his melodies sweeter than ever before on a new flute of bamboo. The cows, the does, the she-wolves and the tigresses generously gave him their milk to drink. Indeed, so much milk flowed that Gitta Ram emptied it all into the pond. And lo! It became a pond of milk!

An old woman was passing by, carrying her earthen pitcher to fetch water. She heard the strains of sweet music, and followed the sound curiously. She was astonished at the strange sight that met her eyes. A small figure dressed in shepherd's robes was seated under a drooping tree by a pond of milk. He played a lilting tune on his bamboo flute, which echoed here, there and everywhere through the wilds. All around the pond were big marble troughs of drinking water for the animals and birds that surrounded him enthralled. She could see even the fish in the pond watch him spellbound from its milky waters.

"Come, mother, fill your pitcher," Gitta Ram beckoned. "This is a pond of milk. Everybody who comes this way drinks from it."

The old woman rubbed her eyes and filled her pitcher, breathless with wonder.

Now the king of that land happened to be wandering nearby. He was hot and thirsty after a long hunt, and had lost his way in the thorny wilds. He saw the old woman and motioned to her to give him a drink from her pitcher to quench his thirst.

"Oh, king!" she bowed low. "Let me take you to a pond of milk. Do you see that yonder?"

The king gaped in astonishment too, at the strange scene before him.

As Gitta Ram played his flute joyfully, the king vowed aloud, "I must catch this wonderful flute player, even if I have to give my life to do it!" And he lunged to grab the tiny figure in front of him.

When Gitta Ram heard the king, he leapt to his feet and began to run. There followed such a desperate chase as has never been seen since in those parts - through bushes and briars and up and down the vast tracts of wild land. Gitta Ram hid himself under the thorniest bushes but the king was determined to catch him. Finally, scratched and badly bruised, the king succeeded in grabbing the elusive flute player.

Just as he did, dark clouds gathered suddenly above and began to thunder menacingly. Streaks of lightning bolted through the sky, while on earth beasts wailed together as though in protest. And then, a plaintive song could be heard clearly above the din -

"Dark clouds, why do you thunder?
Gitta Ram is all alone,
Loving cows, why do you wonder?
Gitta Ram must run from home!"

The sad notes of the song moved the king. He was now astonished to see that what he held was nothing but an anklebone! Slowly, he let it go and left, puzzled and filled with a strange melancholy.

Gitta Ram, the singing spirit went back home - to his little seat under the drooping tree by the milky pond. Once again the melody of his flute filled the air with its sweetness, and cast its magical spell far and wide. And as he played, birds, beasts and fish once again gathered close and listened to him in rapture.

On certain days in the Punjab, when a soft westerly breeze blows, shepherds in the pathless plains may hear the strains of his magic flute, carried in the air. They look at each other then, nod knowingly and say, "Gitta Ram is with us today!" They believe that his spirit will keep watch over them and their flocks always.

Gateway to ancient and medieval India, the historic and prosperous land of Punjab - the Land of Five Rivers, derives its name from two Persian words – *'panj'* meaning five and *'aab'* meaning water. Successive waves of invaders and conquerors over different periods of history led to the flowering of a rich and varied culture here. The fertile plains were the birthplace too of many great religious movements. Hence Punjab has a colourful heritage of folk tales and legends, that may be tragic or humorous.

Its vast plains were cultivated intensively by farmers who toiled all day under hot skies while young boys would drive herds of cattle, sheep and buffaloes to graze. Wolves were very common in the western wilds and this folk tale points to a belief in an invisible shepherd or protective spirit whose flute may still be heard in the plains.

The Donkey Weds Princess Ambika

A STORY FROM HARYANA

KAMLESH MOHINDRA

ILLUSTRATED BY
PULAK BISWAS

Long ago, not far from Delhi, there stood a small village on the border of Haryana and Rajasthan. A poor but hardworking and much respected potter named Saiya lived here.

Saiya had no family except for a pair of faithful donkeys who fetched and carried loads of clay and terracotta ware for their master. Next door lived the young daughter of a washerman, named Radhiya. Radhiya helped the old potter by doing odd jobs for him.

Early one morning, as usual, Saiya woke up and drew water from the well in his yard, had a bath and washed his workshed. He seated Ganapati, the elephant god on his potter's wheel and offered it flowers, vermilion, rice, sweets, and burnt incense.

As Diwali, the festival of lights was around the corner, Saiya had to shape, bake and colour a large number of lamps, altars, little houses and images of Ganapati and Lakshmi, the goddess of wealth.

He was about to start his work when Radhiya barged in excitedly.

"Uncle, come quickly. You have a beautiful grandson! All white, soft and cuddly, unlike any other newborn in the three worlds - heaven, earth and hell!" she shouted, and ran to the donkey shed. Saiya followed her at top speed.

There in the shed stood the proud parents of the baby.

"There can never be more beautiful a baby - even in the kingdom of Lord Indra!" exclaimed the potter with tears of happiness rolling down his brown cheeks. Lovingly, he stroked all the three animals.

"Feed the mother well, Radhiya. And give plenty to the father. He has to do the mother's work as well while she is busy with the baby," said Saiya, wiping his tears with the end of the cotton cloth that was his towel, headdress and a wrap around his shoulders - all in one.

Villagers flocked to the potter's house to admire his special grandson. Their visits kept Radhiya busy serving creamy buttermilk in red earthen cups. Soon there was a hill of used broken cups in the yard, which would be recycled later.

Radhiya adored the new baby and spent most of her spare time feeding and cuddling the little one. When his legs grew a little stronger, he went along with her everywhere. Village children followed him through the cobbled street singing, dancing and clapping.

As expected, the baby grew into a beautiful adult with a fine pair of silky long ears and a voice that could outbray all the donkeys on earth.

One night, while Saiya was asleep, he was startled to hear someone in his room calling out.

"Saiya, oh, Saiya."

He quickly lit his oil lamp and discovered it was his grandson.

"It's me, Saiya!"

"Donkeys don't talk."

"This one does. Watch me, Saiya…" Saying this, he shed his skin, and to Saiya's astonishment a good looking young man in royal robes stood in his place.

He smiled at the gaping potter. "I am Gandharvasen - Lord Indra's son. I broke a rule and my father cursed me. He banished me from heaven to live with the poorest of the poor on earth."

And Gandharvasen went on to tell the potter his strange story.

In the land of the *devas,* young princes and princesses were not supposed to be seen anywhere near their parents' recreation chambers. Once, curious, Gandharvasen peeped through the window to admire a great dancer's performance. She glanced up and missed a step. Lord Indra was angry and wished to know who had distracted the artist and broken the court rule. Finding it was his own son he laid the curse on him.

"That's how I came to be born in your home. I have the power to shed my skin in the night and take on a human form," he ended.

Saiya shed tears when he heard the sad story. He fell flat at the young prince's feet. "Oh, Prince from Heaven! Please let me be of service to you."

"Go to your king and ask him to marry his daughter to your grandson - the donkey."

"But that's impossible! The king will have my head for the insult."

But the donkey did not give up and stood in Saiya's room night after night and pestered him to pay a visit to the palace.

"Saiya, oh, Saiya. Tell the king I could destroy his kingdom if he does not accept my proposal," he said, over and over again.

Saiya was so distracted that he could not concentrate on his work. He just sat by his wheel and did nothing.

"Saiya, why is your yard not filled with goods for Diwali? This is the only season when potters can make money!" the village chief asked him.

Saiya broke down and told him the whole story.

"He is threatening to destroy the kingdom. He might even do it. We should all go with you and beg the king to give the princess to Gandharvasen. We are prepared to die to save the kingdom," said the chief.

A big party of men and women from the village left for the palace.

"Speak up!" ordered the king.

Although it was a cool day, Saiya's loincloth was damp with sweat and clung to his thighs. His knees shook with nervousness. No words came out of his mouth.

The king roared again.

Saiya fell at his feet and asked the king to marry the princess to his donkey.

"He is the greatest of the great donkeys in all the three worlds - heaven, earth and hell!" shouted the crowd of villagers.

"Are you all out of your minds?" roared the king.

"He is threatening to destroy your kingdom. You can kill us all if you wish to. We are going to die in any case," beseeched the people.

"A tricky problem!" the king thought. But soon he came up with a plan.

"Let your wonderful donkey prove himself. He must build a wall, eight feet tall, around my kingdom tonight and finish it before daybreak. Then I shall consider your proposal of marriage," he replied grandly.

"Get up and load me with a sackful of ash. Make a tiny hole at the bottom. Walk me around the kingdom," Gandharvasen commanded Saiya when he heard the king's condition.

The potter and his donkey walked around the kingdom alone in the dark.

Lo and behold! The wall was ready before the first rays of the sun touched the earth. People were amazed but they could neither come in nor go out. There were no openings.

"Only someone gifted with extraordinary powers could do this. As a *kshatriya* I must keep my word and part with my dearest daughter Ambika. Oh, my poor child!" wept the king. Then he sent for Saiya.

"Your donkey is no ordinary being. It pains me much to give Ambika away to an animal - and that too in a poor potter's home. However, you must bring the marriage party to the palace as soon as the astrologer fixes a good time. By the way, your donkey's wall has trapped the whole kingdom. Ask him to make four openings in four directions." Saying this, the king went into his chambers.

Back home, Saiya conveyed the royal orders to Gandharvasen.

"That's no problem. Just load me with another sackful of ash and make four tiny holes in it. Then walk me in four directions," said the donkey. Saiya did just that and like magic four beautiful gateways stood there, dividing the great wall.

On the auspicious date, thousands and thousands of people gathered to witness the strange wedding of the beautiful princess Ambika. Dressed in flowers, bells and glittering clothes, the groom was ushered into the palace. Alongside walked Saiya and his parents, followed by a long procession of villagers. Conch shells were sounded, bells were rung and sweets and coins distributed amongst people. Priests hastily chanted the marriage prayers. And the princess left for the potter's house in a grand palanquin.

That very night the donkey revealed himself to Princess Ambika and told her his secret. Ambika was overjoyed.

Saiya beamed at his royal children and worked hard at his wheel to turn out lots of beautiful things for Diwali.

"Now you don't have to work so hard, Saiya. Ask your donkey's father-in-law to make you rich," the villagers advised him.

"I create pots like a mother gives birth to her children. I pick up a lump of dead clay and bring it to life when I shape it on the wheel. Why should I give up such good work?" he would tell them.

Meanwhile, Radhiya and the princess had become close friends.

"I feel sorry for you, my princess. It must be dreadful for you to be married to a donkey," Radhiya said sympathetically to Ambika as they both sat under a neem tree enjoying fresh tamarind fruit.

"I am the luckiest and happiest woman on this earth," smiled Ambika.

Radhiya could not believe her ears. "There is something here that I do not understand," she frowned. She began to spy on the princess to discover her secret.

One night as she stood by her window, she was amazed to see her beloved donkey shed his skin and turn into an extraordinary human.

"It's unbelievable! He is both prince and donkey! The princess loves the prince dearly. I love my donkey. She may keep her husband. I will take my beloved animal away," she said determinedly to herself, and waited for her chance.

One evening, while Ambika played a beautiful melody on her *veena*, and Gandharvasen listened to her, rapt, Radhiya crept silently into the room. She picked up the donkey's skin and ran out into the darkness. Nobody knows where she went!

Gandharvasen's secret was out! The incredulous villagers were overjoyed that the poor potter's grandson was really a handsome young prince.

Even today potters in Haryana and Rajasthan sing the tale of Saiya and his royal family who lived together happily ever after.

Not far from Delhi, the capital of India, lies the state of Haryana – 'Abode of Gods'. Watered by the Yamuna and several small rivers, this agricultural region, which has a large number of villages, yields abundant crops.

Almost every village has a potter. Instead of a mud hut he may live in a concrete house today, but he would have a well, a kiln fired with cow dung cakes, and the customary wheel. Totally devoted to clay, he still turns out traditional pots. As he works on his wheel, he sings ageless songs narrating charming folk tales of the region.

The Honoured Guest

A STORY FROM MAHARASHTRA

SUREKHA PANANDIKER

ILLUSTRATED BY
SUBIR ROY

Once upon a time, in Maharashtra, a farmer named Gyanoba lived in a village with his three sons and three daughters-in-law. Gyanoba had three acres of land. But the soil of Maharashtra was never fertile, so he could not grow enough on his farm to feed his large family. They were forced to work as labourers in other people's fields. One daughter-in-law would stay back to cook and look after the house while the others went out to work. They took turns to do this.

One day, when it was the turn of the youngest daughter-in-law, a traveller came to the house. He was tired and dirty and there were many wounds on his body.

"Is there any kind lady in the house?" he called from the gate.

"Yes! What can I do for you, honoured guest?" asked the youngest daughter-in-law. She was making a *rangoli* pattern in the courtyard.

"I am a tired and hungry traveller. Could you give me oil and hot water to bathe with and some food to eat?" asked the man.

"Of course! I will heat water and apply oil on your wounds. After that, I'll serve you a meal of *jawar roti* and green vegetables." Saying this, the youngest daughter-in-law put a large vessel on the fire to heat water for the traveller's bath. She applied oil on his wounds gently. After a hot bath, the man felt very refreshed. He enjoyed the simple meal served on a banana leaf by the youngest daughter-in-law.

After the meal he rolled the banana leaf and pushed it under the beam of the roof of the hut. "May God bless you, my child," said the traveller and went his way.

When she went to prepare the evening meal, to her surprise, the youngest daughter-in-law found all the bins of flour and rice in the store full to the brim, and plenty of vegetables in the basket. She cooked a delicious dinner for the whole family.

The next day it was the turn of the eldest daughter-in-law to stay at home and cook. The traveller came again - dirty and full of wounds.

"Is there any kind lady in the house?" he called from the gate.

"Who are you, dirty fellow? And why have you come here?" the eldest daughter-in-law asked rudely.

"I am a tired and hungry wayfarer. Can I get some hot water to bathe with and a little food to eat?" the man requested.

"Go away. There is nothing in the house to give you!" The eldest daughter-in-law shut the door hard in his face.

"So be it," said the traveller, and went his way.

When Gyanoba and the family came back in the evening, there was no food to eat. "What has happened? Why didn't you cook anything?" asked Gyanoba.

"How could I cook anything? All the bins and baskets of provisions were empty. You don't earn enough to feed all of us. What could I do?" the eldest daughter-in-law grumbled. And the family had to go to sleep hungry.

On the third day it was the turn of the middle daughter-in-law to stay back to cook. "Here! I have bought enough supplies for all of us. So have dinner ready when we return," Gyanoba told her. They all left for work.

"Is there any kind lady at home?" Again the same tired and dirty traveller was at the gate.

"Why are you standing here, you filthy creature? Go away!" The middle daughter-in-law shooed him away crossly.

"I will go, but at least give me something to eat," the man begged.

"Go away. There is no food."

"So be it," said the traveller, and went his way.

When the woman went to the store to get flour and vegetables to cook, she found that there was no food in the house.

"Oh, my God! What will I do now? All the supplies my father-in-law bought this morning have vanished!" she cried.

In the evening, when the family returned home, they found her sitting near the empty vessels, crying bitterly.

"What did you do with the provisions I bought? Why didn't you cook anything?" Nobody believed her story about the provisions and vegetables having disappeared.

. Again there was no dinner. Everyone went to bed hungry.

Then came the fourth day. The youngest daughter-in-law was at home again. She heard the familiar voice, "Any kind lady at home?"

"Come in, honoured guest. How are you today? I see you are a little better." She had some flower garlands in her hands.

"No, no! In fact, I have been hungry for two days. And I could not bathe, so my wounds are hurting," replied the traveller.

"It doesn't matter. You will feel better after an oil and hot water bath. And today I will give you some rice and *dal*. Please come in," the youngest daughter-in-law invited him in. She offered the flower garlands to the image of Ganesh she

was worshipping. Then she applied oil to the traveller's wounds. She gave him hot water and put some *neem* leaves in it. The man felt refreshed and comfortable after his bath. And the meal of rice and *dal* was the most delicious he had ever tasted. After the meal he again rolled the banana leaf on which he had eaten his food, and pushed it under the beam.

"May God bless you! May He always keep your bins and baskets of food filled." With that the traveller went his way.

In the evening when the family returned, they were greeted with the delicious aroma of food. There was rice and curry, special vegetables and *puran poli*. All of them enjoyed the meal. As he was drinking water, Gyanoba happened to look up and saw something gleaming under the roof beam. He got up and reached for it. He was astonished to find diamonds, pearls, rubies and gold coins wrapped in banana leaves.

"Where have these come from? Did anybody come to the house?" asked Gyanoba, full of astonishment.

The youngest daughter-in-law told him about the traveller who was tired and dirty and covered with wounds, and how she gave him oil and hot water to bathe. "This was the banana leaf on which I served him a meal of rice and *dal*," she explained.

"You kind-hearted child, it was the Lord himself who came to you! He has blessed you."

"Oh, how I wish I had treated him better when he came!" cried the eldest daughter-in-law.

"I too was rude to him when he came yesterday," the middle daughter-in-law lamented.

"That's why your bins and baskets went empty and we had to go hungry. But the youngest daughter-in-law has truly been blessed," said Gyanoba and his eyes shone with happiness.

The state of Maharashtra lies in the western part of India. The farmers have to toil hard to grow crops here, as the soil is not very fertile. However, the state is industrially developed and is well known for its cultural richness, music, theatre and folk literature. These are an integral part of the daily life of the Marathi people.

Paiyya's Search

A STORY FROM THE DECCAN

INDIRA ANANTHAKRISHNAN

ILLUSTRATED BY
SUBIR ROY

They called him Paiyya. He was just a boy. He lived in the village and he belonged to the village. Somebody fed him and somebody else gave him shelter while some generous soul clothed him. He had no one to call his own. Nevertheless, everybody wanted him around because he was ever helpful.

"Paiyya, get me some vegetables from the market."

"Paiyya, take care of my things while I'm gone."

"Paiyya, get me a bucket of water from the well."

"Paiyya, help me to harvest my mangoes."

Paiyya was always ready to run errands all day long. At the end of the day he was so tired that he slept like a log.

One day, there was a special event in the village. There were many people gathered under the banyan tree in the marketplace. They crowded around a white-bearded man who sat cross-legged under the tree. He was telling them many wise things.

It was a hot day and Paiyya ran in and out of the crowd serving everyone with water to drink. From time to time he stopped and looked at the old man. He did not understand most of what he said. Sometimes the old man sang. Then the crowd sang along with him too.

In the end the old man said, "A guru is a person who will lead you from darkness to light. He will fill your heart with happiness. In this big, wide world, he is the one you can call your own."

The words went straight to Paiyya's heart. His parents had died when he was very young. He belonged nowhere.

"Ah! A guru!" he thought, his feelings of loneliness surfacing suddenly. "Somebody I could call my own! Could I ask this revered man more about it?" he wondered, and looked at him from where he stood, far away.

One by one, the people paid their respects and left. Paiyya waited patiently till the last of the crowd had gone and then he ran to the sage. In a voice quivering with excitement, he simply said, "I want a guru."

The old man looked curiously at Paiyya and laughed lightly.

"It's not easy to find one. It takes a lot of dedication and hard work to reach the feet of a sincere teacher," he said in a serious yet gentle voice.

"Please tell me more," Paiyya persisted.

"You seem to be a tough boy, both in body and mind," said the man, pinching his cheek. Paiyya cracked his knuckles and waited anxiously for him to continue.

"You'll have to go a long way and reach the Vindhya hills, where, long ago, sage Agasthya had his ashram."

"And then…?"

"You will have to search for a true guru there, and do as he says, with pure devotion and faith. He will then be yours forever to inspire and steer you through life."

Paiyya could wait no longer. His mind was already in the Vindhya hills. He fell at the feet of the old man and the next moment he was gone.

The following day everybody was looking for Paiyya. They ran here and there asking one another where he was. There was so much for him to do.

But Paiyya had left the village well before daybreak and was on his way to the hills. As the day grew hotter, the trek became more difficult. He was hungry and thirsty. But he continued walking. When the sun had finished its journey for the day and the chirping of birds had died down, Paiyya reached the foothills of the Vindhyas. His eyelids were drooping with exhaustion as he looked around.

Suddenly he became alert. Just a few yards away sat a man in the lotus pose. His eyes were closed. He had long, flowing hair and was dressed in black. Paiyya's heart thumped like the blacksmith's hammer. His fatigue was replaced with excitement.

"I've found my guru!" he said to himself. He ran and fell at the feet of the man, who opened his eyes a little and noticed Paiyya's dusty clothes and ruffled hair.

"Come, my son," he beckoned to Paiyya and lifted him to his feet.

Paiyya's joy knew no bounds. While he wondered what to do next, the guru opened his eyes, stretched himself and pointed to a large basket nearby. In the fading daylight Paiyya could see plenty of fruit and sweets in the basket. His mouth watered and his stomach rumbled. The guru laughed aloud.

"Eat what you want and have a good night's sleep," he said. And that's just what Paiyya did right away.

The twittering of birds woke him in the morning. The guru was already bathing in the nearby stream. Paiyya did the same.

"Now we will sit and meditate," said the guru when they had dried themselves. Paiyya blinked. He didn't know what to do.

The guru winked at him and said, "Just sit beside me and do what I do."

Paiyya felt uneasy. But there was nothing that he could do. He sat cross-legged beside the guru and closed his eyes. After a short while, he opened his eyes slightly. Devotees were streaming up in a line. They offered a variety of food at the feet of the guru who blessed them. Then they left.

Minutes passed. Paiyya became restless. He opened his eyes wider. The guru's hand came up and shut them.

"Sit quietly and shut your eyes," he whispered to Paiyya. More devotees came and went and then all was quiet for a while. Paiyya was feeling hungry. He opened his eyes a bit and looked at the guru. He saw him open his mouth wide and toss in a *laddoo*. Paiyya jumped and opened his eyes wide.

With a great sly wink the guru laughed and said, "Aren't you hungry? Come, eat what you want. Now that the people have all gone, we are free to do what we want."

Paiyya looked around uneasily. The guru was helping himself to the food in front of him. Paiyya got up, and the next moment, he had taken to his heels. He did not turn or stop till he was totally out of breath and the guru was completely out of sight.

"That was a narrow escape!" he gasped as he slumped down to rest. "I must be careful and look for a true guru."

He continued his long trek up the lonely hill. There was no sign of anybody anywhere. Paiyya plodded along. After a long while, he had almost reached the hilltop when he sighted a small hut and heard the faint sound of running water. He tiptoed up to the hut and peeked inside. A hermit sat with his back to him. A pleasing scent of incense filled his nostrils.

"Who's that?" came the hermit's stern voice.

"How does he know I am here?" Paiyya wondered.

"Speak up and be brief," continued the voice.

Paiyya quickly gathered his thoughts and said softly, "I want to be your disciple." He then waited anxiously for the hermit's reply.

The hermit turned and looked at Paiyya from top to toe. There was something captivating in his deep set eyes which made Paiyya less uneasy than before.

"Hmm! The one thing you must learn as a disciple is obedience. You must do whatever you are told to and never resist," said the hermit in the same stern voice.

"I will never resist," Paiyya replied promptly, and wondered what made him say that to a total stranger.

"Are you prepared to take training?"

Paiyya nodded.

"Well then, your training begins right now. Come with me," said the hermit and led Paiyya to a rocky field nearby.

"See those rocks?" he asked, pointing.

"Yes."

"Remove the rocks from here and stack them behind my hut to make a wall."

Paiyya stifled a gasp. The stones in the field were huge. Carrying them would be backbreaking. As he hesitated, the hermit's disapproving glance alerted him.

He quickly said, "I will do it."

The hermit went back to his hut.

Paiyya looked up at the blue sky. The day was almost half done and the air was clear as a whisper. He took a deep breath and began to work.

Grunting with exertion, he lifted the first rock. As he walked, he balanced it on his shoulder for a while and then put it on his head. He panted with exhaustion and his arms ached with fatigue. He finally dropped the stone at the site with a loud thud and sat on it.

Hour after hour, Paiyya carried the heavy stones and started putting up the wall. There were marks all over his body - bruises, scrapes and even missing fingernails. When the task was done at last, he went up to the hut eagerly, hoping that the hermit would say, "Well done, my son."

The hermit shaded his eyes and examined the stone wall for a while, silently.

He then said, "I don't like the wall there. It obstructs the breeze. Pull it down and bring the stones back to the field."

Paiyya looked at him, aghast. He was about to protest when he remembered his vow of obedience. So, wordlessly, he carried the stones, one by one, back to the field. The hermit watched him while he completed the task.

"Now," he said to Paiyya, "you may make the wall on the front side," and without waiting for an answer, he turned and walked away.

Paiyya felt an intense urge to leave and never return.

"What a guru! This training is nothing short of torture," he fumed. But something held him back and he began to obey the command. The harder the sun beat down upon him, the harder he worked. When the wall was done, the hermit once again came and inspected it.

Suddenly he erupted with laughter. Paiyya was taken aback. While he stood dumbstruck, the hermit said, "I must have been dozing when I gave you my last command. Now I'm wide awake and I can see that this is not what I wanted. Bring the stones back to the field."

For a moment, the world went dark. Paiyya's head reeled and his knees buckled.

"Is this a guru or a demon?" There was a painful lump in his throat and he swallowed audibly. The hermit looked at him sharply while an inner voice said, "Don't worry."

The hermit continued to gaze at him, and the power of his gaze seemed to revive Paiyya. He gathered his wits and said in a trembling voice, "I'll do as you say. But...but, please tell me if you're sure this is what you want me to do finally."

The hermit's eyes seemed to twinkle momentarily. Then they turned fiery as his stern voice said, "Remember, you're breaking your vow by asking me this."

Paiyya bowed his head and looked down at his feet. They were cracked and bloodstained. Just then a cool breeze blew. It seemed to refresh him. With newborn vigour he braced himself to carry out the hermit's instructions. He wanted to be led from darkness to light, he wanted his heart to be filled with happiness, he wanted somebody to call his own.

Without a moment's pause he laboured on. He carried stone after stone back to the field.

Paiyya's energy was draining away. There were just a few more stones to be transported.

He thought bitterly, "I can't drag myself any longer. All this effort is wasted. This task will never get completed." He slumped on the remaining stones, unable to move. A tear crawled down his cheek.

Just at that moment, a wonderful fragrance tickled his nostrils and a soothing hand touched his shoulder. Energy surged from within him and Paiyya jumped up. He heard the same laughter erupt. He reeled around and his eyes met those of the laughing hermit.

The hermit took Paiyya in his arms. Instantly, all his cuts and bruises melted into nothing. Paiyya wriggled out of the hermit's embrace and fell at his feet.

"My training with my guru was not half as simple as yours, you know," confessed the hermit with a mischievous smile as he lifted Paiyya to his feet.

Taking a deep breath, Paiyya remarked, "I can't think of anything that could be more strenuous than this!"

"The path leading to light, happiness and true love is not an easy one," said the guru, and gave Paiyya another great, big hug.

"Now am I ready to tread the path?" asked Paiyya softly.

The guru nodded.

This tale of long ago was narrated to inhabitants of what was then known as the Deccan plateau in the south-central part of India. Sage Agasthya was believed to have had his ashram in the Vindhya mountains. This inspired sages to reside in the region sanctified by him.

Stories relating to these sages and to the ancient guru-pupil tradition were popular in this area and are still enjoyed by young and old alike.

Prince Monkey and Prince Owl

A STORY FROM BENGAL

DIPAVALI DEBROY

ILLUSTRATED BY

SONALI BISWAS

A king reigned over a small kingdom in the plains of Bengal. He had two queens, who were as beautiful as they were kind and gentle. The people of the land were happy under his rule.

Once, the king went on a hunting trip to the hilly tracts of Assam. Near Kamarupa, he chased a rhinoceros that led him deeper and deeper into the jungle and then changed suddenly into a beautiful woman. The king was so overcome by her beauty that he made her his new queen.

The youngest queen was welcomed into the royal palace. The two older queens tried their best to make friends with her. But she wanted to have everything for herself.

Soon after, two princes were born to the two older queens. The new queen used her magic to change the newborn babies into a monkey and an owl. When the king came to look at the faces of his sons she showed him a monkey and an owl, wrapped in red and gold.

The king was shocked and thought his older queens must be witches. He banished them, along with the monkey and the owl.

Wiping their tears, the gentle queens left with their babies. They had been equally shocked to see that they had given birth to a monkey and an owl. But the sons were their own and the two mothers cared for them best as they could. They moved to the outskirts of the kingdom. Some loyal villagers brought them

food and clothes and built them a simple mud hut. The queens were not used to hardship, but gradually they settled down to their new way of life.

The monkey, older by an hour, and born to the elder queen, was named Buddhi-narayan, and called Buddhu for short. The owl was named Bhuta-narayan, or Bhutum for short. Buddhu was frisky and frolicsome while Bhutum was sober and serious-minded.

Just as the two older queens were friends, so were Buddhu and Bhutum. Their mothers hardly called them by their separate names. "Buddhu-Bhutum, your food is ready, get down from the tree and eat," they would call. Or, "Buddhu-Bhutum, it is going to rain. Bring the clothes in."

The villagers got quite used to the sight of the monkey and the owl helping with the household work, gathering fruits and nuts and jumping (or flying) home with them. Buddhu and Bhutum had no idea that they were exiled princes. But one day, a villager remarked, "What horrid luck these princes have - to end up like this!"

Buddhu and Bhutum heard him, and there was no peace in their hearts after that. They went home and accosted their mothers. The two queens had not told them anything about their royal heritage. But Buddhu-Bhutum pestered them so much - that finally they had to tell them the whole story.

"So we are royal princes - heirs to a great kingdom - and you told us nothing!" exclaimed Buddhu. Bhutum just looked reproachfully through his big round eyes.

"Wait," pleaded the elder queen.

"Listen!" cried the younger. But Buddhu bounded out of the house, the courtyard and the village. With a flurry of wings, Bhutum followed.

Away they went, Buddhu jumping from tree to tree, Bhutum on his wings. Soon they crossed the boundaries of that kingdom and the next, going past hills, valleys, rivers and streams. Then came a thick jungle, with marshy land and mangrove trees. It was the Sunderbans, where the Bengal tiger lived. Tired and worn, Buddhu and Bhutum crossed this too. Then Buddhu saw the huts and fields of another land spread out before them, and began to swing merrily from the tree he was on. Bhutum, serious as ever, reminded him that they had yet to sort out the mess they were in.

Meanwhile, the queens were crying their hearts out for Buddhu-Bhutum. They called and called, looked in every tree, and all around the village. Finally,

there was nothing to do but to wait. The two women often went to bathe in the river that flowed by the village. On the bank, there was a grove of plantains. Each queen would pluck the petals of the plantain-flower and make a boat out of them and put some food on it – a few nuts and berries, and push the boat onto the river to flow along with the waters.

Buddhu's mother would sing,

> *"Buddhu, my son!*
> *What wrong did I do*
> *that you left me in sorrow?"*

And Bhutum's mother would sing,

> *"Bhutum, my son!*
> *What wrong did I do*
> *that you left me in sorrow?"*

The petal-boats would float away, bearing the fruits and nuts and their tears. But as Buddhu-Bhutum were sitting on a tree discussing their problems they caught sight of a man aiming an arrow at a nearby tree. Buddhu leapt onto a higher branch to get a better view. A pair of parrots was sitting there, almost hidden in the green leaves. But they had not been able to escape the hunter's eye. Buddhu signalled to Bhutum and he swooped down upon the hunter and began to peck at him. In the same instant, Buddhu jumped on him and began to bite and scratch. Dropping his bow and arrows, the hunter fled.

"That was brave," said one of the parrots. "He could have turned on you."

"That was kind," said the other parrot. "You need not have bothered about us."

Buddhu-Bhutum felt pleased.

"We overheard you talking about some problem," said one of the parrots.

"Tell us, you look so tired and worried," said the other.

"Tell you!" grinned Buddhu. "What good would that do?"

But Bhutum narrated their whole story. And soon Buddhu was glad he did. For the parrots spoke out, "We too have a story to tell. We are not parrots. We are princesses Roopkumari and Phoolkumari from Kamarupa."

"Isn't that a long way off?" asked Buddhu.

"Isn't that the place the new queen came from?" asked Bhutum.

The parrot who was named Roopkumari said, "We belong to a distant land. Our father wanted us to marry a prince from Bengal whom we did not fancy at all. He came on a visit to Kamarupa with his mother and we knew there was something wrong with him. You see, we know some magic ourselves."

Buddhu was so surprised that his tail stood on end. Bhutum took it more calmly and asked, "Did you use that magic on yourselves?"

"Yes," Phoolkumari said. "Our father was set on our marrying that fellow. He filled the palace with guards and soldiers. So we turned ourselves into parrots and flew out of the window."

"So you see we may be able to help you," said Roopkumari. "It is possible that you are not animals at all but human beings, and I can undo any spell the new queen may have cast on you."

Bhutum's round yellow eyes shone as he agreed. "Yes, if you know the reverse spell."

In reply, the parrots broke out into a long cackle. Buddhu-Bhutum shivered and trembled all over, and suddenly they found themselves – no longer monkey and owl, but princes in shining armour and jewelled headgear! Buddhu was as impressed to see Bhutum as Bhutum was to see Buddhu. They held their shields out before them and were impressed with their own reflections too.

But the parrots broke out into another long cackle, and in a few moments, turned into two beautiful princesses in silken clothes and precious jewellery.

All four would have gone on staring at each other, but a tiger roared and they were jolted back.

"We must go back and claim our kingdom," said Buddhu.

"But do we know the way?" asked Bhutum.

"I don't," said Buddhu. "I just leapt from tree to tree, not in any particular direction."

"Neither do I," admitted Bhutum. "I flew along with you, and didn't take note of the way."

They trudged through the dark forest, going they knew not where. Soon the armour started to feel heavy and the silk began to catch on thorn-bushes. Tired and sweaty, they passed through the Sunderbans.

The marshes gave way to firmer land. This meant they were going back the way they had come. But they could not be sure. Footsore and hungry, the four sat down to rest beside a small stream flowing by.

"Travel was easier when I was a monkey," grumbled Buddhu.

"Talk sense," Bhutum began, then suddenly asked, "What's that?"

Something was floating down the stream, maroon in colour, with fruits and berries on it. Behind it, there was another little boat made of plantain-petals.

Buddhu and Bhutum guessed the boats were sent out after them by their mothers because they bore their favourite fruits and berries. The fruits were rotten and the berries wrinkled, but both Buddhu and Bhutum were overjoyed.

Now they knew the way back. They went upstream along the banks and soon the stream widened into a river with villages and fields along it. They recognized the land they had grown up in. Buddhu and Bhutum were home!

The queens were sitting alone in their hut when the two princes rushed in, crying, "Ma!" It took the queens some time to understand what had happened. When they did, they could hardly speak for joy. The princesses were given a warm welcome also.

The next day, all six of them set off with a band of loyal villagers to the king's palace. The king was on his throne, the new queen by his side. Close by, in splendid royal dress, stood her son, none other than the prince the two princesses had been asked to marry!

Recognising their old queens, the palace-guards allowed them in. The elder one swept up to the king with Buddhu and said, "Your son, Buddhi-narayan – no monkey." The younger one swept up to the king with Bhutum, and said,

"Your son, Bhuta-narayan – no owl."

Meanwhile, Roopkumari and Phoolkumari quickly worked their magic, and before anyone in the royal court knew what was happening, a huge rhinoceros appeared where the new queen had sat and another where her son had stood.

The court was thrown into utter confusion. Guards and soldiers rushed in and killed the two rhinoceroses with their spears. The king gave a tremendous start, as if he had woken up from a long sleep. He folded Buddhu and Bhutum into his arms.

Prince Buddhi-narayan took Roopkumari for his wife, while Prince Bhuta-narayan got married to Phoolkumari. The older queens were back at the palace. Happy at last, their dark days over, they sang a different song.

The older queen would sing,

> *"Buddhu, my son!*
> *What right did I do that you came back*
> *and I have no sorrow?"*

The younger would echo,

> *"Bhutum, my son!*
> *What right did I do that you came back*
> *and I have no sorrow?"*

And so they all lived happily ever after!

This story is set in Bengal, which included what is now Bangladesh, before India's independence. An eastern state, Bengal is bounded by the Himalayas on the north and the Bay of Bengal on the south. This region is lush and green, fed by many rivers. The Sunderbans are forests on the delta of the river Ganga where it flows into the Bay of Bengal and home to the Royal Bengal Tiger.

Further to the north-east is the state of Assam. Assamese women, especially from Kamarupa, were thought to have magical powers. The monkey and the owl are quite common in Bengal. In Bengali, 'buddhi' means intelligence, but 'buddhu' means idiot. But here 'Buddhu' is applied to the monkey as a term of endearment. 'Bhutum' is a common variety of owl in Bengal.

The Sun and the Moon

A STORY FROM JHARKHAND

Amrita Bogra

ILLUSTRATED BY
Jagdish Joshi

In the beginning of Time, much before you and I, only the Sun shone brightly on all of Creation, constantly covering the world in its golden light. There was no Moon. Only the hardiest of life forms could survive as the Sun's rays beat down relentlessly from a clear blue sky.

Then one day the Sing-Bonga, the greatest of all the Santhal gods, came down to Earth for a visit disguised as an ordinary man. He stopped beside a settlement of thatched huts nestling at the edge of a forest. Cries rose from the centre of the clearing as the women busied themselves over skinning a wild pig. Bare-limbed children played in the dust. Here and there a dog flicked at flies half-heartedly with his tail, before seeking out the cool of the shade. A hunting party was returning from the forest. Now and then they stopped to forage for edible berries and fruit, stuffing them into their woven leaf baskets, to carry back to the village.

A little distance away from his hut, a farmer was busy digging in his field. Walking towards the farmer, the Sing-Bonga noticed that while many of the fields appeared freshly dug, others looked ready for planting. In some, the tender leaves of tubers were already peeping greenly out of the soil.

"When did you prepare this field for sowing?" he asked, as the farmer paused for a drink of water from a gourd that lay at his feet.

"Just now," replied the farmer, wiping his face on his arm as he bent down to pick up his stick. "Would you like a drink?"

"No, thanks. And what about those fields over there?" enquired the Sing-Bonga, pointing to some fields a little distance away.

"Oh! Those...they were prepared just now too," answered the farmer, returning to his digging.

The Sing-Bonga was puzzled. His gaze fell upon some fresh leaf plates.

"When did you eat from these plates?" he asked the farmer curiously.

"Just now," replied the farmer tersely, without stopping his work.

Then the Sing-Bonga pointed towards some dried leaf plates lying beside another field. Once again he asked the same question, and got the same reply.

"But when do you work, and when do you rest?" the Sing-Bonga exclaimed, even more puzzled than before.

"All at the same time," shrugged the farmer. Unwinding the long strip of animal hide that he wore on his head for protection from the sun, he paused to mop his dusty and sweat-begrimed face. Then he took another gulp of water.

"There is, you see..." he continued, as he prepared to resume digging, "there is no time other than the present."

The Sing-Bonga decided to go on a world tour to see, at first hand, what the situation was in other parts of the world. He travelled far and wide to all the four corners of the Earth. Everywhere he went, he saw that mankind toiled ceaselessly, and, everywhere, all of Creation was covered in hot sunshine all the time. He realised that he must think of a plan by which work periods and leisure time would be clearly defined. He thought awhile. At last he snapped his fingers and his face broke into a smile.

"I know what to do now!" he exclaimed aloud to himself. "I shall make 'night', and that is when mankind shall have all the time to relax and rest."

He returned to the village and sought out the farmer who was, still, busy digging in his field. The farmer looked up curiously as the Sing-Bonga approached.

"I have decided to make 'night' for you," announced the Sing-Bonga briskly, coming straight to the point, "and that is when I want that you should relax and take rest."

"Night?" asked the farmer in wonder. "I do not understand - what do you mean by 'night'? And, by the way, if I may be bold enough to ask - who are you?"

The Sing-Bonga just smiled at the farmer and vanished. He then sent for the Sun.

"Because you shine all the time, mankind continues to work on and on, and if this carries on, he will die of exhaustion. Obviously this state of affairs cannot be allowed to continue. Now listen to me carefully - for this is what I want you to do. Divide your time equally between the times that you shine from those that

you don't. When you set, and darkness falls, man will have to rest. And, by the way," continued the Sing-Bonga, "I also wish you to regulate the intensity of your rays so that all of Creation gets some respite from your searing heat."

"It shall be as you command, Great One," replied the Sun.

From that day hence the Sun began to set in the evening. Night covered the face of the earth. Man was filled with wonder. Unable to see in the darkness, he stopped working at sunset.

All of Creation breathed a sigh of relief as, in the coolness of dawn, song birds greeted each new day. Animals crawled out of their burrows, which they had dug deep in the earth to escape from the searing heat of the Sun, to roam the Earth freely, taking shelter only at noon when the Sun blazed brightly in the Heavens.

The Sing-Bonga paid a visit to the farmer again.

"Well," he asked, "now do you know what I meant when I said that I would make 'night' for you? By all means work as hard as you wish during the day – but when night falls you must rest. This is to be the pattern of your life. Work and rest."

The farmer then realised, at last, that he was in the presence of the Sing-Bonga himself.

"I understand, oh Great One," he whispered, bowing low before him, "and I shall do as you have commanded. But there is one small problem...."

"And that is...?" asked the Sing-Bonga kindly.

"Well, Great One," began the farmer slowly, "it is true that I stop working at dusk, but as I have to return home in the darkness, I have often fallen into ditches and hurt myself. More often than not, I am covered with bruises. Please tell me, how may I return home safely to eat and rest?"

Once again the Sing-Bonga realised that the changes he had brought about were incomplete. Something more still needed to be done for mankind.

"All right," he said at last, "I shall arrange for the Moon to shine for you at night."

Saying so he vanished; but since then the Sun and the Moon have shared the Heavens to bring light to mankind.

The Santhals are a colourful tribe of Jharkhand, the state carved out of south Bihar. They are also found in the neighbouring districts of Orissa, Bengal, Assam and as far south as Kerala. They believe in 'bongas' and magic. Living in complete harmony with their surroundings - the hills, dales, springs and the sacred groves of *sal* trees - they have no temples or idols. Their Supreme Deity is known by various names – 'Sing-Bonga', 'Thakur Jiu' or 'Marang Buru'. There are twelve clans among the Santhals. Each has a distinct totem.

The Merchant's Daughter

A STORY FROM ASSAM

MIRA GARG

ILLUSTRATED BY

SUDDHASATTWA BASU

Once there was a merchant in Assam who had a beautiful daughter named Tezimola. Not only was Tezimola very beautiful, she was also very good. Unfortunately, when she was a child, her mother fell ill and died. As her father was often away on long trips for work, Tezimola was lonely and had no one to take care of her. Hence he married again, so that his daughter would have a mother and someone to look after her.

Tezimola's father loved her very much. But her stepmother turned out to be very cruel. She made Tezimola do all the work in the house and treated her like a servant when her father was away. She beat her and scolded her whenever she got the chance. Tezimola was very unhappy. She often cried quietly, but always tried to do what her stepmother wanted her to do, without complaining.

Slowly, Tezimola grew up to be a beautiful woman. Her stepmother was jealous of her beauty, for she had large eyes like a deer and a complexion that was milk and honey. Her long black hair cascaded down her tall, slim body. Her laughter and voice were like music to the ears. But poor Tezimola was seldom given a chance to laugh.

One day Tezimola wanted to go to Rupohi's wedding. Rupohi was her closest friend. They had shared many things in their childhood. When they were young girls, Tezimola found solace from all her sorrows in Rupohi's company and a shoulder to cry on.

Rupohi's wedding was something to look forward to, but Tezimola's clothes were not fine enough for the occasion.

She went to her stepmother and said, "Oh mother, I want to go to my friend's wedding, but I have no nice clothes to wear. Can you lend me a pair of your good *mekhla chaddars*?"

"Certainly, Tezi," her stepmother said, "but you must take proper care of them."

"Of course, I will," Tezimola replied gratefully.

Tezimola was very happy and excited, and looked forward to her friend's wedding. She took the package her stepmother had given her, containing the dress to be worn at the wedding, and left home.

When she reached her friend's house, she opened it up to change. To her dismay she found there was a piece of hot charcoal in the folds of the dress. It had burnt a hole in the *mekhla*. Tezimola started crying with fear and disappointment, dreading what her stepmother would do to her when she found

that the dress had been ruined. She could not figure out how the coal had got into the package. Innocent as she was, she did not realise that her stepmother had planted the coal between the clothes.

The marriage was over. Tezimola went home. When her stepmother saw the condition of the *mekhla chaddars* she was furious. "You careless girl! Can't you ever look after anything? You will be punished for this. You will have to put both your hands, your feet and your head in turn, into the grinding slot in the granary when I pound the grain."

Poor Tezimola's hands and feet got badly injured when her stepmother pounded them hard, several times. Then she was asked to put her head in the slot. This was the last straw. Tezimola's head broke and she died.

The stepmother then threw Tezimola onto the rubbish heap at the back of her kitchen.

Days passed. One day, an old woman walking by asked the stepmother if she could pluck and take a few of the sweet gourds growing behind her kitchen. The stepmother told the old woman that there was no sweet gourd plant in her backyard. But when she looked she realised she hadn't noticed the plant growing there. She told the old woman to pluck the gourds and take them.

When the old woman stretched out her hand to reach for the gourds, a voice called out, "Do not pluck me, do not pluck me. I was killed and thrown here by my stepmother. I am Tezimola!"

Hearing this both the women were taken aback. The old woman fled hastily, thinking there surely must be a ghost there.

But the stepmother was terrified. In a panic, she pulled the plant by the roots and threw it over the fence by the side of her garden. But the roots remained in the backyard and being in a hurry, the wicked stepmother did not notice this. She thought she had got rid of the plant.

Many days passed. One evening, at sunset, a handsome young man passed by. He stopped short when a sweet fragrance filled the air. Looking around, he noticed an exquisite, solitary white flower that gleamed in the fading light. He bent to take in the fragrance and inhaled long and deep. Never before had he smelt or seen anything so beautiful. Desirous of taking it home, he put out his hand to pluck it. Suddenly a voice broke the stillness.

"Do not pluck me, please...do not pluck me! I am not the beautiful flower that deludes you. I am Tezimola. I was killed and thrown here by my stepmother!"

Bewildered and disturbed, the young man retreated. All the way home, the fragrance and the voice haunted him, leaving an unforgettable impression on his mind. He resolved to get to the bottom of this strange event.

The next day it began to rain heavily and did not stop for three days. The whole garden was flooded. The beautiful white flower was torn and broken by the storm and swept away to a pond by the gushing rivulets of water. This pond opened out into a stream and the flower was carried away to the river.

After some time the weather cleared. The sun shone and its reflection on the waters quivered like a plate of gold. Fishermen came out with their boats in the hope of making a good catch.

Meanwhile, Tezimola's father was returning home by boat. As he was crossing the stream, he saw a lovely lotus flower growing in the water.

"I will take this for my Tezimola," he thought. He asked the boatman to pluck it.

As the boatman reached out for the lotus flower, a voice cried out, "Do not pluck me, do not pluck me! I was killed and thrown here by my stepmother. I am Tezimola."

The boatman was frightened. He hastily withdrew his hand and told his master he could not pluck the flower as there was a spirit there that spoke.

So the merchant himself went to pluck it. Again the same voice repeated the same words, adding, "I am your Tezimola…"

The merchant was perplexed. He uprooted the whole plant, took it home and put it on his windowsill. Then he asked his wife, "Where is Tezimola?"

His wife lied, "She has gone to spend some time with her friend."

The merchant was not convinced. He went back to his room. There he found that the lotus plant he had placed on the windowsill had become a bird. He took his *gamucha* and placed it tenderly on the bird. Moving away a little distance, he said, "If you really are my Tezimola, come fly towards me and become your real self again."

The bird flew towards him and transformed itself into the beautiful Tezimola again. Both father and daughter held each other close and shed tears of happiness.

The mysterious disappearance of Tezimola had perplexed all the people of the village. Now word spread that Tezimola was back home again.

One day, months later, a young man came by to ask if anyone by the name of Tezimola lived in that house. He had travelled far and wide in search of her. He narrated to the merchant the story of the fragrant flower and how it had haunted him. The merchant was touched by his concern and, in turn, narrated all the sorrow and suffering his daughter had been through. He called for Tezimola. The visitor was dazzled by her beauty.

"I will never let her suffer again," declared the young man, and asked for her hand in marriage. He then revealed his true identity as the prince of the neighbouring kingdom.

Tezimola and the prince were married. The stepmother was banished from their household for being so wicked and cruel. Everyone was happy, and there was peace and harmony all around, especially for the good and beautiful Tezimola and her father.

This story is from 'Asom', the original name of Assam, which means 'peerless'. Assam lies to the northeast of India, a lush, green, fertile land, as old as the *Puranas*. The ancient city of Pragjyotishpur, 'the light of the east' (now the bustling city of Guwahati) was a centre of learning and enlightenment, and scholars and wise men came here from far and wide.

Assam is thus a rich amalgamation of different cultures, whose visual legacies still remain in many parts to this day. Its vast fund of myths and legends are a treasure trove for the imaginative and the creative mind.

Buying a Song

A STORY FROM MADHYA PRADESH

VINITA KRISHNA

ILLUSTRATED BY
ATANU ROY

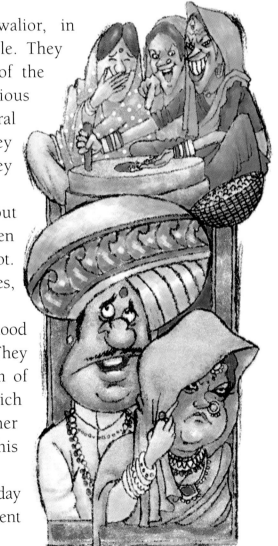

In a village called Ghatigaon, near Gwalior, in Madhya Pradesh, there lived a rich couple. They had all the luxuries possible. The lady of the house possessed beautiful saris and precious jewellery. They owned many acres of agricultural land. In short, the couple had everything they could wish for, except for common sense. They were both simpletons.

The village women would often gossip about the rich woman's simple-mindedness and the men poked fun at the rich man, every chance they got. This made the rich couple unhappy and at times, even angry.

Each morning, the women in the neighbourhood would grind their corn and wheat into flour. They would make up songs and sing to the rhythm of their grinding stones. This would make the rich woman very jealous, because she could neither make up songs nor sing in tune. And this invariably made her a target of ridicule.

Fed up of being the butt of their jokes, one day she decided to ask a neighbour for help. She went

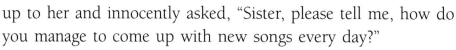

up to her and innocently asked, "Sister, please tell me, how do you manage to come up with new songs every day?"

The neighbour was a crafty woman and thought it was a good opportunity to fool the rich woman, so she sniggered and said, "My dear, didn't you know that songs are sold in the market? Why don't you just go and buy some?"

The rich woman got very excited when she heard this, and anxiously waited for her husband to return home. As soon as he entered, she told him what the neighbour had said and asked him to go and buy lots of songs for her from the market right away. The husband was astonished. He told his wife that he had never heard of such a thing.

"You must be mistaken," he said. But she would not listen and told him that she had to have the songs by the evening or he'd be sorry. "I don't care how you get them!" she added.

The rich man was perplexed. He had no idea where one could buy songs. "What a bizarre thing she is asking for!" he said to himself. However, he knew that he had to go and look for them, otherwise his wife would not let him have any peace.

So he set off for the market. On arriving there, he entered a shop and enquired, "Do you sell songs?"

The shopkeeper was flabbergasted. He had never had such a strange request before. He decided to have some fun too, and said to the rich man, "I'm sorry, sir, my stock of songs has just got over. Why don't you try the next shop?"

The shopkeeper at the second shop played the same trick and sent the rich man to the next shop. In this way he went from shop to shop, looking for a song but couldn't find any. By the evening he began to get worried. He knew that his wife would not let him sleep in peace if he did not return with a song for her, but he didn't know where else to look. Tired and anxious, he started to walk home.

On the way, he noticed a big rat running across his path. Struck with curiosity, he followed it to its hole in the ground. When he got there, he heard a peculiar sound coming from it. After listening for a while, he realised that it was the sound of the rat digging in the hole. The sound had an interesting rhythm and it gave the rich man an idea. Trying to imitate it, he said aloud,

"Scrapety-scrape, it claws and digs!"

He liked the way it sounded and kept repeating it to himself as he walked along. Some distance ahead, he saw a black snake slithering across the road. And the moment he set eyes on it, another line came into his head:

"Slither, slither, it slips and slides!"

The rich man liked the second line even better. He repeated both the lines together:

"Scrapety-scrape, it claws and digs!
"Slither, slither, it slips and slides!"

He was overjoyed now, as he had two lines of a song with him.

Further ahead, the rich man spotted a rabbit peeking out of a bush. As he went closer, he was amused to see the rabbit looking here and there in fear. And another line popped into his head:

"Hither, thither, in fear it peeps!"

As he repeated it aloud, the frightened rabbit jumped up and ran back into the bush. The rich man laughed and said:

"Up and down, it hops and leaps!"

He was thrilled, for he had a full song now! He repeated the lines over and over again as he made his way home.

When he reached home, the rich man's wife asked him, "Did you bring any songs for me?"

"Oh yes, I did!" he said. "I have got one song for you."

"Why only one?" asked the woman, a little disappointed.

"It is a very expensive song," lied her husband, trying to save his skin. "It is a very precious song and so when I tell you about it, you must memorise it and not let it slip from your mind."

The woman listened attentively as her husband taught her the lines of the song. She repeated after him:

> *"Scrapety-scrape, it claws and digs!*
> *Slither, slither, it slips and slides!*
> *Hither, thither, in fear it peeps!*
> *Up and down, it hops and leaps!"*

She liked the lines but was a little confused. She asked her husband, "This song has no tune. How will I sing it?"

"Listen, my dear," said her husband, "I have spent all my time and money getting you these four lines. Now you will have to think of a tune on your own." Exhausted, he went off to sleep.

The rich woman was quite pleased with the song and wanted to make sure that she wouldn't forget it. So she lay down and kept on repeating it in bed. She was unable to sleep as she tried to think of a tune for the lines.

In the middle of the night, while she was struggling to find one, she heard the faint sound of someone whistling outside. She put her ear to the wall in order to hear the whistling better and then tried to sing out the first line of her song to its tune.

"Scrapety-scrape, it claws and digs!" she sang out loud. Little did she know that at that very moment, two thieves were digging a hole in the wall, trying to break into their house, and the whistle that she had heard was actually a signal for one of them to start digging. When she sang the first line to the tune of the thief's whistle, she liked the way it sounded. She became very excited and began to sing out the line again and again.

Hearing her, the thief who was digging a hole in the wall was alarmed at first. Then he dismissed it as a coincidence, and began to crawl into the hole slowly.

Inside, the rich woman began to sing the second line.

"Slither, slither, it slips and slides!" she crooned.

The thief, suspicious now that he was being watched, began to look around nervously. At that precise moment, the rich woman, inspired by her success, sang out the third line heartily.

"Hither, thither, in fear it peeps!"

The thief was quite sure now that the lady had seen him and was trying to alert the men of the house to go and get him. He decided to make a run for it. He jumped up, and as he did so, the woman sang out the next line with all her enthusiasm.

"Up and down, it hops and leaps!"

The thief, scared stiff that he'd be caught, ran and gave himself up to her. He dropped to his knees and began to beg her, "Forgive me lady, please let me go."

Shocked at the sight of a strange man barging into her room, the woman screamed. Her husband woke up and caught the thief quickly. By then it was morning and, hearing the commotion, the entire neighbourhood collected in front of their house. Once the thief had been handed over to the constable, curious, the rich man asked his wife what she had done to make the thief surrender to her.

Innocently, she said, "Nothing. I was simply singing the song you had bought for me from the market yesterday."

The husband put two and two together and realised what had happened. He decided to make the most of this coincidence and spoke out, loud enough for everyone to hear, "Ah! What a clever song I purchased for you!"

All the villagers were impressed that the song had scared the thief away from the village and one of the women said, "I think this is the best song in the entire village." Everyone in the crowd agreed and from that day onwards, they began to treat the rich couple with respect.

Even today, the women of Ghatigaon grind wheat early in the morning and sing while they do so, hoping to ward off evil and bring in joy and prosperity.

Madhya Pradesh is known as the heart of India. This state is located in the centre of the country and was perhaps the oldest dwelling place of human beings in India. Excavations here have revealed a cultural sequence right from the Stone Age to the early historical period. The state is partly hilly, part plateau and part plain. The Vindhya mountains stretch across it while the Narmada river flows through it. The Chambal belt of north Madhya Pradesh is full of zigzagging ravines which provide shelter to notorious gangs of dacoits.

The Sacred Drum

A STORY FROM ARUNACHAL PRADESH

VIJAYLAKSHMI NAGARAJ

ILLUSTRATED BY
SONALI BISWAS

A long time ago, when God created the universe, it was totally desolate. The raging waters of the mighty oceans covered everything. There was only darkness and the divine power of God.

Then God commanded, "Let there be light!" and created day and night. He created Donyi, the Sun, which shone brightly during the day, bringing life all around, and Polo, the Moon, which shone through the night with serene calm. This was followed by the creation of the earth, plant life in all its variety, colourful birds and animals and finally God's most wonderful creation, mankind.

Men began to worship God in the shape of the Sun, Donyi, and the Moon, Polo, as well as other gods and goddesses.

But one day, it is believed, a devastating storm shook the earth, destroying everything that came its way. The winds blew, there was heavy rain and big hailstones knocked down much life.

A few people managed to survive the storm. Among them were a brother named Khimwa and his sister Tunka. Khimwa toiled all day – farming, hunting and fishing to find food for both of them.

Once he decided to go and look for a wild boar with some friends. All day they roamed the hot and humid forests, but did not find a single boar. Tired and disappointed, Khimwa sat down by a pond thinking that they would have to go hungry that night.

Then, suddenly, a strange sound came to his ears. "Dum-dum da-da, dum-dum!" It was the rhythmic sound of a *dhol* being beaten and it came from somewhere close by. Unconsciously, Khimwa began to tap his feet.

"Can you hear that?" he asked his friends. "Listen!" The sound of the drum mesmerised him; it seemed to revive his spirits, making him forget his worries.

"Where is this sound coming from?" he wondered. "Why does it make me feel so good?" He got to his feet.

He noticed a huge tree with a large trunk growing at the edge of the pond. The sound seemed to be coming from there. As he stood there listening, it stopped for a while, and then began again, "Dum-dum da-da dum!"

"I think it's coming from inside the tree!" he exclaimed. "I must find out!"

"No, wait," said one of his friends. "There might be a spirit inside the tree which is making this sound."

But Khimwa was most eager to find out and rushed towards the tree. As he got closer, he noticed that there was a spear lying just next to it.

"Why is this spear lying here?" he asked.

"Don't touch it!" warned his friends.

Khimwa didn't listen and touched the spear cautiously. "If there is a spirit inside, it might come out if I pierce the tree," he said. He picked the spear up and aimed it at the tree.

Just as he was about to push it in, a gentle voice said, "Son, why do you want to pierce the tree? Don't destroy this lovely tree."

Khimwa turned, and was surprised to see a beautiful female figure standing there. There was something so riveting about her that he was left spellbound and speechless.

"I am the goddess Khilli Manmi," she said. "Tell me, son, what made you come here?"

"These drum beats drew me here - they mesmerised me and made me forget all my troubles," Khimwa replied hesitantly, looking at the serene face of the goddess. "I wish I could create the same music."

"Your wish shall be granted!" said the goddess. Suddenly she produced a vast array of drums, big and small, some intricately shaped, some plain and simple. "Choose any," she said.

Khimwa gazed at them fascinated. Then he pointed to one. "That wooden drum, so beautifully decorated with beads and feathers and shells, is all I want," he said.

The goddess smiled. She picked up the drum he had selected and gave it to Khimwa.

"You have made a good choice," she said. "This is a sacred drum and its music has great power."

"Thank you, holy one," Khimwa bowed low. "I shall play this during the Mol festival to worship Donyi and Polo."

"Remember one thing," said the goddess. "You have to take good care of this drum. Like all sacred objects it must be treated with great respect."

"I promise, I will," Khimwa said, bowing his head reverently. "It will be the most precious thing for me."

When the Mol Festival came, Khimwa slung the drum around his neck and played it while people worshipped Donyi and Polo. His drum beats had such a captivating rhythm that there was magic in the air when he performed. They seemed to say, "There is joy in living in love and peace. Come, let us dance and pray." And all the people responded to them.

Year after year, Khimwa was chosen to play the drum during the Mol festival. Young and old danced with happiness and Khimwa lovingly cared for the sacred drum. He cleaned it every day, wiping away even the smallest speck of dust, replacing the beads, shells and feathers when they became shabby.

The fame of the sacred drum spread and Khimwa was invited to play it in villages far and wide. But as time passed, his fame began to go to his head. He became proud and arrogant and forgot that the goddess had gifted him the drum and that her blessings were behind its power.

"Ah! I am the greatest player ever born! It's my magic hands which produce these drum beats that captivate everyone," he boasted.

Soon he began to neglect the drum. He did not bother to clean it or replace the beads when they dropped off or the feathers when they became crumpled.

When the Mol Festival came around again, Khimwa dressed up in his best festive clothes as usual. He took out his drum, dusted it carelessly and set off.

Large crowds of people had come to take part in the festival. There was gaiety all around. Khimwa waited with his drum slung around his neck, and soon the time came for him to play.

His hands danced over its sides with their usual practiced ease. The people waited expectantly around, ready to begin their dance. But to Khimwa's horror, no sound emerged. He tried again and again, till his hands ached, but the drum remained silent. The mesmerising beats had vanished! The people gazed at him shocked, then slowly moved away, murmuring amongst themselves. The Mol festival lost its life, and nobody celebrated with the same joy.

Khimwa walked away, overcome with gloom. Worse, in the coming months, a large number of misfortunes befell the people and many felt it was because the sacred drum had stopped playing. Without the enchantment of the drum beats Khimwa's life became meaningless. He stopped speaking and his sister became very worried.

All the time he wondered - how did his fingers lose their magic? Why had the drum stopped playing? One day, he took it out sadly and looked at it. Suddenly he realised how shabby it had become. He remembered what the goddess had told him and was overcome with shame.

Khimwa decided to pray to the goddess and ask her for guidance. When she did not respond, he wooed her with different offerings. He searched for the most beautiful flowers and the juiciest fruits in the forest. "Forgive me, holy one," he prayed. "I have sinned. I am sorry...I really am."

After Khimwa had prayed for a long time, the goddess finally appeared.

"Khimwa, you have shown true devotion," she said, blessing him. "What can I do for you?"

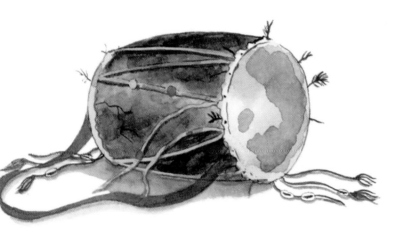

Khimwa bowed his head. "Oh Khilli Manmi, please make my drum produce music again. I will do anything you say. The drum, my music, is my life. I grew too proud. I should have looked after it," he wept.

"I am pleased to see you repent," the goddess said. "I shall give your drum a new lease of life. But you must repair it, decorate it more beautifully. And remember...you must not forget to look after it," she added.

Khimwa slowly lifted his head and then fell on his knees. "How can I thank you, holy one?" he cried. "I promise to look after it and play even better!"

He redecorated the drum with the most colourful beads and the brightest feathers he could collect in the forest.

And then, gently, he tapped on it. "Dum-dum, da...da!" The sound had come back! He leapt with joy.

Khimwa began to beat the drum again, slowly at first, then with great vigour. He played and played till his fingers ached.

And then…the Mol Festival came again, and the preparations began. Khimwa lovingly decorated the drum with goat fur, boar's teeth and feathers from the hornbill to please the goddess.

The magic beats resounded far and wide as the celebrations began. "Bless our community and our village," Khimwa sang. "Bless the birds, the animals, the flowers and plants. Let there be plenty to eat for all!"

The entire village participated in the festival with great joy.

Khimwa had only one thought now, to create pure music and spread harmony by playing the sacred drum. He continued to play it for the rest of his life.

The snow-topped mountains along its northern boundary, the meandering river Siang, the tall pines and rhododendrons of Kameng, the austere grandeur of the Lohit valley, and the gentle woods and green fields of the Apatani plateau – all make up the beautiful land of Arunachal Pradesh.

The Sun, Donyi, and the Moon, Polo, are important to the people of Arunachal, as they worship them. They believe that all the creatures on this beautiful earth were created by the invisible spirit of God personified in Donyi and Polo. The people of the Muklom tribe get together in a common place to worship Donyi and Polo during the Mol Festival. The word 'Mol' signifies prosperity to people, the well-being of all animal life and a good harvest.

The Disbelieving King

A STORY FROM ANDHRA PRADESH

BILKIZ ALLADIN

ILLUSTRATED BY
SUDDHASATTWA BASU

Once, long, long ago in India, there was a kingdom which was renowned as much for its good king, as for its wise minister. It was a prosperous kingdom, with wide roads on which bullock carts could travel easily and large shady trees, so that travellers could rest under them when they were tired. There were plenty of fields too, where rice and wheat were grown, so the people had enough to eat.

The king was a fine looking man. He had dark, sharp eyes, an aquiline nose, and a moustache which curled up at the ends. He wore lots of jewels over his robes, rings on his fingers and jewelled armlets.

His greatest asset, however, was his minister. He was a wise and god-fearing man. He would offer prayers devoutly every morning and pray for the king and his people. Then he would say, "We shall leave the rest to God. If we ask Him, He will surely advise and guide us. I know that whatever He decides for us will be good. We should leave everything in His hands."

"Should we build a fort here, or make another road?" the king would ask. "Do you think building a wall here will make us safe, just in case anyone decides to attack us?"

The minister would think, look at the maps and plans and reply, "Yes, Your Majesty. We shall do what we think is best for us and leave the rest to God. He knows what is best for us. If we trust Him, He will not let us down."

The king did not really believe his minister, but he humoured him and did not argue with him.

The king was very fond of hunting. One day, he decided to set out for the forest with his minister and a few courtiers. It had rained for some days and the dust had settled, the sun was out and it seemed to be an ideal day for being outdoors. They were riding fast when they saw some beautiful deer. They gave chase, and as they were nearing their quarry, a rock came sliding down the hillside. The king did not see it. Suddenly, his horse reared and he was thrown to the ground. The rock fell on his left hand and he cried out in agony.

His courtiers jumped off their horses at once and ran to lift up the rock.

The king was in great pain. He was most annoyed with his courtiers for not saving him. He was very angry with himself too. "I have such sharp eyes!" he cried. "How is it I did not see that rock? What shall I do now?"

"Let us ride back quickly to the palace, Your Majesty," the minister said, "so that the physicians can attend to your thumb."

They hurried back to the palace. The *vaids* looked at the king's thumb and shook their heads grimly.

"It has been very badly crushed," they said. "We will have to amputate it."

So the king's thumb was amputated. Not only was he in great pain, but sad, angry and annoyed with everybody and everything as well.

"What will happen now?" he cried in agony. "When will this heal? Oh, when will this thumb of mine be all right?"

"It will heal soon, Your Majesty," the minister said comfortingly. "It will heal soon."

"Yes, but I'll look so horrible!" the king roared back. "A king with no thumb! Why did this have to happen to me? O-oh, a-ah!" he screamed with pain.

"God alone knows," the minister replied. "Perhaps it is all for the best."

"All for the best? What do you mean by that?" the king cried angrily. "I lose my thumb and you say it is all for the best!" And he dismissed the minister in rage.

But the king was not happy. He walked up and down in his rooms like an angry, caged tiger. Nobody dared to come near him or speak to him. Even the queen and princes kept away. He was disturbed because he had dismissed his minister but he did not want to call him back. He did not want to discuss the kingdom's affairs with any of his courtiers, who he felt were not clever enough. So he managed everything by himself.

Some months went by and the king's thumb healed. There was no pain but he had to get used to the idea of having a left hand without a thumb, though every time he looked at his hand he felt angry and sad.

Then one day he decided to go hunting again. He was well now and wanted to ride, so he set out. But this time his minister was not with him. Nor did he take his courtiers along. He went all alone.

As luck would have it, some fierce tribals were roaming in that area at the time and they captured the king. They took great fancy to his royal bearing, to his jewels and grand clothes. In their own language they told each other that this man would be the right person for their sacrifice.

And they started to prepare for it. They built a fire, and hammered poles into the ground. Then they caught the king and tied him fast to the poles.

In vain did the king plead with them to spare him! He was so frightened that his teeth chattered, and perspiration streamed down his face.

"Let me go," he begged. "If you let me go I will give you lots of jewels and money." But they would not listen.

"I shall give you whatever you ask for," he tried again. But they continued chanting and beating their drums.

Then suddenly, one of the tribesmen screamed and pointed to the king. The others stopped their chanting and beating of drums and gathered around the king to see what was wrong. The man pointed to the king's hand. He lifted it up, showing everybody the four fingers, frowning and shaking his head as if he were saying the king was not perfect. He had no left thumb.

The men shook their heads too and untied the king. They seemed to be saying, "This man will not do. We need a human being who is physically perfect for our sacrifice."

The king noticed his horse standing near a tree. He ran, leapt onto its back and quickly made his escape. He did not stop or look behind till he reached his kingdom.

When his people saw him return, they broke into cheers of joy. But the king did not wait and went straight to the palace. He headed for his room where he fell on his knees and thanked God for saving his life. By then his people had gathered around the palace to see him. Special prayers of thanksgiving were offered. The queen and the princes garlanded the king to welcome him back.

The king was happy and relieved at his narrow escape. He sent for his minister right away.

"I must acknowledge my mistake," he said. "If I had not lost my thumb, I would have lost my life, and would not be here today. You were right! God knows what is best for us, and it is better for us to leave things to Him." He embraced the minister and said, "You are a good and wise man."

The king installed the minister in his old position again and everyone was happy in the kingdom once more.

This story is from Andhra Pradesh in south India. The state is bordered by Tamil Nadu in the south, Karnataka in the west, Orissa in the north and the Bay of Bengal in the east. Telugu is the language spoken here. Andhra has a rich cultural tradition of dance, music and folklore and was once ruled by many powerful dynasties. The traditional practice of kings being guided in matters of state by wise ministers is highlighted in this story.

The Tests of Friendship

A STORY FROM PUNJAB

SANTHINI GOVINDAN

ILLUSTRATED BY
TAPOSHI GHOSHAL

Once upon a time, there lived a partridge in a forest. Since she was a small and rather frail bird, she felt that it would be useful for her to make friends with a larger and stronger animal who would be able to protect her. She visited a jackal who lived nearby.

"Dear Jackal," she said, "will you be my friend? I need a strong and powerful ally like you to help me fight my battles."

The jackal however, was a vain and mean creature, and he immediately replied, "Of what use will it be to me to be friends with such a small and helpless creature like you? My idea of a friend is someone who can make me laugh, and who can make me cry. A true friend will be able to provide me with a good meal, and will even save my life if required! You couldn't possibly do any one of those things, so you can never be my friend!"

"Why don't you give me a chance to prove myself?" asked the partridge.

The jackal agreed.

"Follow me!" cried the partridge excitedly.

The partridge flew on till she spied two travellers walking along a dusty road. They were tired and hungry. The partridge flew

enticingly above the turban of one of the travellers. Immediately, the other traveller, seeing the plump bird, decided that he would try to catch it for his dinner. He hurled one of his shoes at it. The quick bird dodged the flying shoe, but it struck the head of the first traveller, who whirled around furiously.

"Why are you hurling your shoe at me, you rascal?" he cried, seizing the second traveller by his collar.

"I was not hurling my shoe at you," cried the second traveller indignantly. "I was trying to catch a partridge that was hovering over your head!"

"Well, then, where is that partridge now?" demanded the first traveller angrily. But the clever partridge had flown out of sight.

The two angry travellers fell upon each other and began to fight furiously, raining blows and tearing each other's clothes to shreds. The jackal, who was watching from a distance, began to laugh heartily.

"Are you satisfied that I can make you laugh?" the partridge then asked the jackal confidently.

"Well, you certainly made me laugh," said the jackal readily, "but I doubt if you can ever make me cry!"

"Hide in the hollow of that big tree there, and just watch me!" cried the little partridge.

The partridge waited till she saw a hunter with his pack of dogs coming along the road. She flew close to the dogs, flapping her wings hard to attract their attention. When they began to chase her, she flew quickly to the tree hollow where the jackal was hiding.

As soon as the dogs smelt the jackal, their noses quivered, and they began to bark and growl ferociously, as they scratched the bark of the tree furiously where the jackal was hidden. The terrified jackal began to cry loudly and piteously.

As the partridge heard his cries, she smiled. She flapped her wings and quickly caught the attention of the dogs once more, and soon she had lured them back to their owner.

When the partridge returned to the tree hollow, she called out triumphantly to the jackal, "Haven't I proved to you that I can make you cry too?"

The shaken jackal agreed, but he said, "After putting me through that terrible ordeal, you must prove your friendship to me by providing me with a good meal. Then I promise you that I will reward you with my friendship!"

"Done," said the partridge happily. "Watch me carefully! I will provide you with a chance to have a hearty meal. All you will have to do is to help yourself!"

The partridge waited till a group of women came down the road, carrying baskets filled with food that they were taking to their husbands. She then lay on the side of the road, fluttering her wings feebly.

"Oh, look!" one of the women cried as they noticed her. "A wounded partridge! We will be able to catch her easily!" She threw her basket down, and ran towards the partridge. As she approached, however, the cunning bird leapt up and flew a little distance away. Then she pretended to be hurt again, and lay down, fluttering her wings.

"Help me catch that partridge!" the woman cried out excitedly to her companions. They all threw down their baskets and ran to help her. The nimble partridge however kept tricking them, and led them a merry dance. The jackal, seizing his opportunity, crept up to the unattended baskets and stole as much food as he desired.

When he had finished his meal, the partridge asked him, "Well, are you satisfied now?"

"That was certainly a superb meal!" said the jackal, smacking his lips in delight. "But even though I enjoyed it immensely, I cannot give you my friendship yet because you have still not passed the ultimate test of friendship - you have not yet proved to me that you can save my life!"

"No, I haven't," replied the partridge. "But it is growing late now, so it is better that we return to our homes in the forest. It will take us a very long time if we go walking back on the road, so let us cross the river. I know a crocodile who will carry us across on his back."

Accordingly, the jackal and the partridge set off for the river. They sat comfortably on the crocodile's broad back, but just when they were right in the middle of the swollen river, the partridge said to the jackal, "I think that the crocodile is planning to trick you! Just imagine how terrible it would be for you if he were to drop you into the river!"

"Well, it would be equally terrible for you," replied the jackal.

"Not at all," replied the partridge airily. "You forget that I have a pair of wings with which to take flight!"

The jackal turned pale. Just then the crocodile, who had been listening to the conversation, spoke up. "I might just devour you both, you know."

"Oh, we know that you could never do that," replied the partridge quickly. "That's why we agreed to ride on your back! I would fly away the moment you try to catch me, and as for my friend the jackal, he is too smart to bring his precious life with him when he comes out. He keeps it well under lock and key at home!"

The crocodile was taken aback. "Is that so?" he asked doubtfully.

"Yes!" cried the partridge. "You can try to eat him if you like, but it will not be possible and you will only wear your teeth down in trying!"

The crocodile was so amazed by this thought, that he did not utter another word, and he carried his passengers safely to the riverbank.

"Well, what do you have to say to me now?" the partridge asked the jackal when they were alone. "Aren't you satisfied that I can save your life?"

"My dear Miss Partridge, you have made me laugh and made me cry. You have provided me a good meal, and even saved my life. But I'm sorry; I'll never be your friend! You are much too clever for me, and I'll keep out of your way forever!"

And the jackal did just that!

The northern state of Punjab is the granary of India. A land of ancient civilisations and epics, it is the cradle of the ancient Indus Valley. The people of Punjab are warm and fun-loving with a legendary capacity for hard work and enterprise. They love to sing and dance, the energetic and rhythmic *bhangra* dance is very popular all over. Punjab is rich in arts and crafts, and Punjabi cuisine is world-renowned. Stories from this state mirror the energy and enterprise of its people.

A Forest Friend

A STORY FROM UTTAR PRADESH

Somya Dave

ILLUSTRATED BY
Tapas Guha

The forest was to the south of the tiny plot, separating it from the main village. A few mango trees, some vegetables growing in a sunny corner and dark green vines creeping lazily over the thatched roof of the little hut in the middle - this was five year old Gopal's little world.

The village women sometimes dropped by, but Gopal and his mother mostly stayed alone.

Things had been different when his father was alive. His mother spoke little of her grief, but she didn't sing any more while milking the cow or churning yoghurt in the big earthen pot. Using a well-worn rope, she would twirl the wooden churner rapidly, spraying Gopal's face with delicious little splashes of frothy buttermilk. The soft, creamy white butter that floated slowly to the top was scooped into a small pot, which hung from the rafters. After being heated slowly over a fire, it made fine *ghee*, aromatic and clear golden in colour.

Their cow and her calf were tethered to the mango trees by nightfall. Usually their gentle mooing and the sound of tinkling cowbells was all the music Gopal needed to nudge him to sleep. But for the past few nights he had trouble shutting his eyes and clung tightly to his mother for comfort. Whenever he did close them, the familiar dread of the dark forest came rushing back.

The forest had never frightened Gopal earlier. He had grown up playing in the nearby groves. He knew well enough that the beloved cowherd Krishna, who had grown up in these parts of Vrindavan, had vanquished all the demons that had preyed on man and beast alike.

Gopal had listened in awe too to how Krishna had danced on the many hoods of the great sea snake Kaliya, until heeding the anguished pleas of the snake king's wives, he had permitted the entire clan to return to the ocean.

His mother had tried to calm his fears. "Son, you know that there aren't any fierce beasts around these parts."

But she obviously hadn't seen the dark places where the sunlight could scarcely pierce through the treetops, thought Gopal. Nor could he convince her about the large yellow-black snake he was certain he had spotted in the undergrowth. The raucous cries of a flock of peacocks often startled him into thinking that a herd of stampeding elephants might be coming his way.

"I'm sorry you have no friend to accompany you on the trail," his school teacher had said kindly. He had heard how the little boy would stop every now and then to check for demons and peer for snakes, panting as he raced to school, too hot and tired to pay much attention to his lessons!

Gopal's mother had hoped that he would overcome his fear in a few days. But now the sight of his small, pinched face as he dressed for school, was too much to bear.

"Come here, Gopal," she called to him. "Have you met your kinsman in the forest yet?"

"Uh, what kinsman?"

"I must be growing old. I quite forgot to tell you about him. He's just a couple of years older than you and a real handful. He scampers through the forest with his cows and then goes around stealing butter and teasing the village girls!"

Gopal's eyes lit up. "Can I meet him, Mother?"

"You'll probably hear him long before you see him…he plays entrancing melodies on his flute."

"How do I find him?"

"Just yell out 'Gopal, Gopal' loudly in the forest grove near the bank of the Yamuna river."

"But why should I call for Gopal? That's my own name, Mother!"

"Because he's your namesake, my dear! You know *Go – pal* means 'keeper of the cows'. He has all the makings of a fine herdsman…"

"But - will he talk to me, Mother?"

"Of course, he will. Just smile and introduce yourself and I'm sure you'll be friends in no time."

So it was a cheerful Gopal who strode towards school that day. Back in the hut, his mother murmured, "You'll look after my little one, won't you, Gopal?"

"Gopal! Hey *Gopaaal* ! Where are you, my kinsman?" Little Gopal stood perplexed in the dark thicket. He yelled again, "I know you're hiding somewhere to escape a scolding. I won't tell anyone about you. And I'm not scared, so you can come out now."

He waited long and slowly tears welled up in his eyes. "If you don't come out, I'll never be friends with you, ever!"

The minutes passed. Still he stood and waited. "I'm not going to school today, do you hear, and it'll be your fault! Don't blame me if you get a good scolding."

A slight breeze had sprung up. It carried the soulful melody of a bamboo flute.

"Now I know you're there. Come on out. Quick!"

The bushes parted. Out came a dark skinned boy, with twinkling eyes and a wide, naughty smile. He had tucked a few peacock feathers in his headband and held a bamboo flute in his right hand.

"Hey, is that you scaring my cows away with all that shouting?"

"Are you Gopal, my kinsman? I'm also called Gopal! And it's not my fault. I wouldn't have yelled so long if you had answered me sooner!"

"Yes, I am Gopal and if you say I'm your kinsman, I'll just take your word for it! I was tending to my flock on the river bank. That's quite far from here, you know."

"But what do I call you? Calling you Gopal is too confusing," asked little Gopal.

The older boy threw his head back and laughed loudly.

"That's true! Do you know my family and friends call me by a thousand different names? You can call me Mohan if you like. It's simple."

Mohan and Gopal soon became friends and the little boy eagerly looked forward to meeting his friend in the forest, twice each day. They chatted and laughed and Mohan taught him how to play a simple tune on his flute. Gopal's beaming face convinced his mother and teacher that he no longer feared crossing the forest. But he didn't tell them anything about Mohan, worried about getting him into trouble.

The days went by. Soon it was time for the school feast. All the students

looked forward to this holiday when special home-cooked delicacies were shared with the school teacher and friends - all except Gopal. He was dreading the feast day. The cow had died last month and he couldn't bear to ask his mother to give him a pot of rice pudding for school.

"Why are you so glum this morning, Gopal?" asked Mohan.

"Err…it's nothing. It's just the school feast today."

"And that's a sad event, is it?" laughed Mohan.

"No, it's just that I have nothing to take to school."

"Oh, but you do have something to take. Look here," said Mohan, holding out a tiny dish heaped with some rice pudding.

"That must be your breakfast. I can't take that."

"Oh no! I drank so much buttermilk this morning that I can scarcely eat a spoonful. Go on, take it. It's really good."

"Thanks, Mohan. You're my true friend!"

The teacher looked at the little dish that Gopal held out proudly, with barely enough rice pudding for one person.

"This looks so good that I'll eat it all myself."

Gopal smiled with delight.

"But of course, Sir. I'll be really proud if you enjoy it."

"That's the best rice pudding I've had in my life!" declared the school teacher.

"If you'd really liked it you would have eaten it all up," said Gopal, crestfallen. For the tiny dish was still brimming with rice pudding.

"What! But I just finished it off!" Glancing down at the dish the schoolteacher couldn't believe his eyes.

"There must have been a little bit left over. I'll take some more."

But the dish still brimmed with rice pudding.

"Maybe I'll give some to Bhola. Here, come here, son. Bring your plate."

But still the dish stayed full. Long after all the school children had eaten their fill there was rice pudding for all the villagers. Such a tiny little dish and food for over a hundred people!

Gopal giggled with delight. It was that lovable rascal Mohan up to his tricks again. At first he had watched equally amazed but had soon realised that this was no ordinary breakfast dish, but a very special gift from his best friend.

The school teacher soon coaxed Gopal to tell him the entire story.

"Can this be true? This Mohan can be none other than Lord Krishna! He chooses to reveal Himself to this little boy while I've prayed to Him all my life and never yet heard from Him. Take me to the forest, my son. Krishna! Krishna! I'm coming, my Lord!"

The school teacher picked Gopal up in his strong arms and ran towards the forest, followed by the entire village, chanting praises of the Divine Herdsman who had blessed them with food from his own house.

"Mohan, my friend, won't you come out and meet these people? They're so funny, they think my best friend is the great Lord Krishna!" Gopal spoke loudly as the crowd listened in silence.

A soft, melodious voice spoke out from nowhere in particular.

"Dear Gopal, I am indeed your friend Mohan. But I am also the same Damodar Madhusudan to whom your mother prays, and Krishna for these villagers. I am whatever my devotees wish me to be. But you alone Gopal, of all these good people, called out to me with such faith and love that I had to come running to meet you. My blessings are with all these people. But only you have earned the privilege of being my friend."

Little Gopal thought that his heart would burst with happiness. That rascal Mohan had had the last laugh after all!

The legendary forests of Vrindavan in the north Indian state of Uttar Pradesh were Krishna's playground.

An incarnation of Vishnu, Krishna was believed to be the nephew of the murderous king Kansa of Mathura. Smuggled out of prison to live with foster parents who were cowherds, Krishna became the beloved of the local people. The region abounds with stories of his mischievous pranks and exploits, and it is difficult to separate myth from reality.

The area around Mathura and Vrindavan, also known as Braj Bhoomi is very popular among pilgrims, and is well-known for its temples, fairs, festivals and handicrafts.

Tapoi

A STORY FROM ORISSA

VARSHA DAS

ILLUSTRATED BY

JAGDISH JOSHI

In a coastal town of Orissa there lived a merchant who was so rich that he was known as the Merchant-King of Orissa. He was adventurous and ambitious. His business was spread all over the Indian sub-continent and beyond. A large fleet of beautifully carved ships carried his merchandise to be sold across the seas, and brought back rare items from other countries to trade in India. Since he had little competition, his business flourished.

The Merchant-King had a large family - parents, grandparents and eight children. He and his wife cared for all, old and young, with respect and affection. Their first seven children were boys while the eighth was a beautiful daughter named Tapoi. Since they had longed for a girl, everyone in the family showered their love on Tapoi. If she asked for one flower she would get ten. If she sneezed, the whole household would be at her service!

The Merchant-King educated his sons well and trained them in his trade. As they grew up, they began to help their father in his business. They were so efficient that the father gradually passed on all his responsibilities to them. The seven sons began to travel in seven different directions and their business flourished even more.

As the sons came of age, they got married. The house became livelier with the addition of seven cheerful and hardworking wives. As for Tapoi, she was delighted to have seven sisters-in-law. Being the only girl she had often longed for female company and was particularly fond of the youngest.

One day when Tapoi was away at school, the seven sisters-in-law were sitting together in the garden. Suddenly, the eldest said, "Don't you think our husbands pay too much attention to Tapoi?"

"You're right," agreed the second one. "My husband doesn't even look at me when she is around."

All except the youngest echoed the same feelings of anger and jealousy. But they knew they could not do anything. Their husbands and parents-in-law would not tolerate anyone raising even an eyebrow against Tapoi! They decided to wait for an opportunity to settle scores with her.

Time passed and the Merchant-King and his wife grew old and died, within a space of six months. Tapoi and her brothers were inconsolable. But the brothers took extra good care of Tapoi so that she would not miss her parents.

Now after the period of mourning was over, the seven brothers set off on business. Tapoi's sisters-in-law grabbed this opportunity. Together they made a plan to get even with her.

Once again the eldest took the lead. "Tapoi is stealing our share of love and attention from our husbands. Let us teach her a lesson."

"Yes," agreed the second one. "We must not miss this opportunity."

"She thinks far too much of herself. We should cut her down to size," added the third. All the others had something nasty to say about Tapoi, except the youngest. Though she was intimidated by her older sisters-in-law, she mustered the courage to say, "Tapoi is the youngest and the only sister. It's natural that her brothers should pamper her. Why should we envy her? She has a place in her brothers' hearts and we have ours."

The eldest sister-in-law pounced on her. "Keep quiet. Don't pretend to be so virtuous! She is like the princess of the house and we are like her servants! We can't tolerate this any more. Let's send her to graze the goats in the jungle. She'll either lose her way or be eaten up by wild animals."

"That's a brilliant idea," the other five agreed. However, the youngest felt very troubled. She was warned to keep her mouth shut else she would be thrown out next.

Tapoi was summoned and ordered to take the goats to the jungle to graze before sunrise. She was stunned. She had never fetched even a glass of water for herself! But she had no choice but to obey her sisters-in-law.

The next morning, the eldest sister-in-law pulled Tapoi out of bed and pushed her out of the house with the goats. Tapoi followed them into the dense forest with dragging steps. The goats began to feed happily but Tapoi shed bitter tears. She had no food, no water. Fortunately, the goats were used to going in and out of the forest every day and led Tapoi safely home at sunset.

The sisters-in-law were surprised to see her back. Normally they never counted the goats when the shepherd brought them home, but that day they decided to do so. Unfortunately for Tapoi, one goat was missing. It happened to be the eldest sister-in-law's favourite. She roared with anger, "Go back to the jungle and don't return till you find my goat!"

Tapoi pleaded with folded hands, "It's so dark and the jungle is dense. I'll go in the morning and find your goat. I am very hungry and tired."

"You will not get any food till you find my goat!" The sister-in-law pushed her out roughly.

Tapoi returned to the jungle. She could hardly see in the dark and kept walking wherever her feet took her. Suddenly she stumbled over a small rock, hurting her foot. When she sat down, she was astonished to find that this was not an ordinary rock but a statue of the goddess Mangala!

At once Tapoi apologised to the goddess for having touched her with her foot. Her youngest sister-in-law had secretly tied a handful of rice in her torn sari. Tapoi quickly untied the knot and offered the rice to the goddess. Goddess Mangala was the protector of young girls and Tapoi felt a little better. But when she remembered her sisters-in-laws' cruelty she couldn't help crying.

Full of sorrow, Tapoi called out to her brothers for help, even though she knew they were so far away that her cries would never reach their ears. After a while she saw a young man walking towards her with a torch in his hand. When he came close, Tapoi recognised him with joyful surprise and ran to hug him. He was her youngest brother! Hearing the cries of a young girl, he had come to her aid. He could never have imagined he would find his beloved sister here.

Tapoi's brother took her out of the forest to the sea-shore where the older brothers were anchoring their boats. Horrified to see Tapoi dressed in tattered clothes, they brought her new clothes immediately and fed her with their own hands. When Tapoi had eaten to her heart's content, they asked, "Why are you in this state? What were you doing in the jungle at night?"

Tapoi broke down again. She did not wish to speak ill of her sisters-in-law. But when her brothers insisted, she narrated the whole story. The brothers were furious. One of them suggested that their wives' noses be chopped off and they be thrown out of the house. Another said that Tapoi should punish them severely. But Tapoi was happy to be with her brothers again and did not wish to take any revenge.

Then the youngest said, "Tomorrow morning our wives will come to the sea-shore to perform the welcome ceremony. They will worship the boats. We will anchor one a little away from the shore. Tapoi will sit in it, dressed in the most beautiful sari and ornaments. We'll tell our wives to go to that boat one by one, and worship the goddess sitting inside."

"That's a brilliant idea!" said the other brothers, but the eldest one was still so angry that he told Tapoi, "When they enter the boat and bow before you, hit them hard on their backs with a stick. Don't forget how much they tortured you."

Tapoi was too kind and forgiving to pay back her sisters-in-law so cruelly. But she agreed to sit in the boat dressed like a goddess. She thought it would be fun!

The next morning, the seven wives reached the shore to welcome their husbands. They enquired if they had had a safe voyage and if business had been good. The brothers did not reply but asked curtly, "Where is Tapoi?"

The eldest wife looked at the others, cleared her throat and said, "She was not feeling well so we asked her to rest at home."

Now the brothers exchanged glances. The eldest one said, "Oh! That's too bad! You had better finish your ritual soon so that we can meet Tapoi."

Pointing at the boat anchored a little away from the shore, the youngest brother told his eldest sister-in-law, "We have brought a magnificent life-sized idol of a goddess. Please go to that boat one by one, and seek her blessings."

The eldest sister-in-law wanted to show how obedient she was. She ran into the water, climbed onto the boat and went inside. Tapoi was dressed very beautifully and her head was partially covered, so her sister-in-law could not recognize her. She fell at her feet and said, "Please bless me with all the good fortune in the world. I have got rid of Tapoi at last. Please protect me from my husband's wrath."

Tapoi placed her hand on her sister-in-law's head and said, "May you repent and be happy."

Tapoi's voice struck the eldest sister-in-law like a thunderbolt. She fell flat on the ground in a faint. Then the second sister-in-law arrived. She pushed the eldest one away so she could touch the goddess' feet and seek her blessings. Her prayer was similar to the elder one's. Tapoi repeated her words, "May you repent and be happy."

Tapoi's voice hit her like a hammer. She too fainted. In this way six sisters-in-law went to worship the goddess and fell flat on the floor of the boat.

Finally the youngest entered. She was stunned to see the others lying unconscious at the feet of the goddess. She went close, but before bowing she looked at the goddess' face.

"Tapoi!" she exclaimed. Tears of joy welled up in her eyes as she hugged her dear Tapoi. Together they came out of the boat and went home with the brothers, leaving the others there.

The sisters-in-law gained consciousness towards the evening, and they could have died of shame. Hesitantly, they returned home. When they reached, their husbands scolded them severely for their cruel actions.

But Tapoi came to their rescue once again. And then they realised how foolish they had been to be so jealous, and to hold Tapoi responsible for their husbands' indifference. They begged Tapoi to forgive them.

Tapoi's words echoed in the air, "May you repent and be happy." And they all lived happily ever after!

Orissa is situated in the eastern part of India. Its borders touch four different states. West Bengal and Jharkhand lie to its north, Chhattisgarh to the west and Andhra Pradesh to the south, while the Bay of Bengal provides a large coastline on the east. The people and the language of the state are known as Oriya.

The Oriyas have been adventurous seafarers and have traded with far eastern countries for centuries. Many melodious folk songs are sung about their lives away from home. There is a special festival in Orissa to worship boats before they set sail after the monsoon. The sea beaches of Orissa attract tourists from all over the world.

The Promised Boon

A STORY FROM BIHAR

PAULOMI MISRA

ILLUSTRATED BY
SUJATA SINGH

A long time ago, in Monghyr in Bihar, there lived an old woman. She was very poor. The only person she could call her own was a son whom she had lovingly named Rajan. The only earthly belonging she could call her own was a mud hut with a thatched roof, which lay next to a big, shady neem tree. In the hot summer days, the thatched roof was covered with creepers from which bitter gourd, ridge gourd and white pumpkin hung in abundance. These were nature's gifts to her.

The old woman toiled all day long, grinding grain for people, sweeping floors and doing any other menial chores that she could get. In return for her work, people would give her grain and other eatables with which she fed her son and herself.

Our story begins one evening when the first showers of the season had made the atmosphere hot and humid. The rain was persistent and it was still pouring heavily when the old woman returned home with a handful of broken rice grains and pulses that the village head's wife had given her for cleaning their huge cowshed.

She lit an oil lantern carefully and washed the rice and pulses with water from an earthen pot. Then, she lit a fire for cooking, with dry wood. She had collected this earlier from the forest and stacked it in a corner of her hut. It came in handy on rainy days like this when the twigs lying under trees were wet and unfit for lighting a fire.

Next, the old woman lovingly put a pan on the fire to make her son's favourite dish, *khichdi*.

Just when the *khichdi* was ready, a bearded mendicant knocked at her door.

"Mother, it is raining heavily. Please give me some food and shelter," he pleaded.

"I have no food to give you," replied the old woman. "This *khichdi* is for my son. He will be home any moment. I am sorry. I cannot help you."

The holy man would not take 'no' for an answer. He appealed to the old woman's sense of hospitality and promised to give her a boon if she fed him.

Tempted by the idea of receiving a boon, the poor woman quickly served the *khichdi* to the mendicant. He ate heartily and got ready to leave as soon as the rain stopped.

"Your son can come to me and I will grant him the boon," he smiled and left.

Rajan soon returned home and asked his mother for food. She told him about the holy man's visit and his promise of the boon in return for the food and shelter.

His hunger completely forgotten, Rajan flung a towel over his shoulder and immediately went out in search of the mendicant.

He walked down a dirt track along the swelling Ganga, and leaving the village and fields behind, he finally found himself in a dense *sal* forest. The forest was silent and dark. Rajan continued walking with cautious steps. He could hear twigs snap underfoot. The rain had not been able to penetrate the thick canopy of the *sal* trees.

Soon night fell and Rajan was tired. He thought it would be best to rest. He sat down under a tree and looked around. When he glanced up, he realised that he was sitting under a mango tree that looked withered and dry.

When the mango tree saw Rajan, it asked, "It is late at night and the forest is dense and dangerous. Why are you here at this time?"

"I am in search of a holy man who is like God to me. He has promised me a boon."

The mango tree was thoughtful for a while. Then it said, "Can you please also ask your God why I am withering?"

"I will surely do that when I find him," Rajan replied, and soon fell asleep.

The next morning, Rajan woke up full of vigour, plucked a *datun* from a neem tree and cleaned his teeth. Then, he took a dip in a nearby stream. He wiped himself with his towel and wore his clothes. Completely refreshed, he resumed his journey.

Suddenly, he heard the sound of an elephant trumpeting in pain.

Startled, Rajan turned to his right. A little distance away, he saw a huge black elephant with big white tusks.

"I wonder what makes the elephant trumpet so loudly," thought Rajan, who loved animals.

Gathering courage, he walked up to the elephant. He was surprised to see that the elephant was in pain because its trunk was stuck in the branches of a huge *sal* tree.

"May I help you free your trunk?" Rajan asked the elephant.

"It's no use," replied the elephant. "I have been trying to free myself for a long time but my trunk seems to be stuck fast."

Before Rajan could say anything more, the elephant asked, "Where are you going, my boy?"

Rajan told the elephant about the journey he was making in quest of his God.

"Oh! Then I think you can help me," said the elephant. "Can you also ask your God why I am suffering so much?"

"I will certainly do that," promised Rajan, and continued on his journey.

In a few hours he had crossed the forest and entered a kingdom. The people there seemed very prosperous and happy. However, Rajan found out that despite all the prosperity, the king was unhappy.

Rajan saw the king standing near a bridge, which must have been a very big and lofty one but had now fallen to the ground.

When the king saw Rajan, he took an instant liking to him. He took Rajan to his palace and served him a lavish meal. After a while he told Rajan that the bridge he had seen earlier was erected every day, but at night it would just collapse! No one was able to find out why.

"This is the problem we are facing," said the king. "But what brings you to my kingdom? May I do something for you?"

"My quest for my God has brought me to your kingdom. He has promised me a boon," Rajan told the king.

The king thought awhile and said, "Then, can you do me a favour? Can you also ask your God why the bridge we build every day collapses each night?"

"I will do that," promised Rajan. Thanking the king for his hospitality, he continued his journey in search of God.

In the evening, Rajan reached a mountain range. In front of him stood a high rocky mountain that he would have to climb. It was growing dark and Rajan had to decide whether to stop at the foot of the mountain till the next morning or to continue his journey.

"I still have half an hour of daylight," he thought. "I will make good use of it and climb the mountain."

The mountain was formidable, but Rajan was not deterred. He started climbing, one steady step after the other. Soon he had reached the mountain top. He was surprised to see a bearded sage there, sitting cross-legged, deep in meditation.

As Rajan did not want to disturb the holy man, he walked silently past him. Suddenly, the man opened his eyes and looked at Rajan.

"Son, what brings you here?" he asked, getting up.

Surprised and a little frightened, Rajan bowed his head and replied, "I am looking for my God who has promised to grant me a boon."

"Then, son, you have come to the right place," smiled the holy man, and placed his right palm on Rajan's head.

As soon as the sage's palm touched him, Rajan saw the whole mountain begin to glow. He sensed joy and peace like never before. Immediately, he fell at his feet and begged him for the promised boon.

"Go home, my child," said the holy man, "and you will find the boon as you travel back home."

Touching his feet once more, Rajan asked him the questions the mango tree, the elephant and the king had told him to ask.

"The mango tree has ten pots of gold coins hidden in its root," replied the holy man. "The tree has been greedy and hidden the pots so well that no one has ever been able to take even a single coin. Once the pots with the gold coins are removed, the tree will flower."

"The elephant should have been dutiful and carried men on his back. He did not do so. He failed to help anyone," continued the sage.

"As for the king, he has a daughter who is very beautiful and intelligent. The king is so proud of her that he believes no groom is worthy of her. So, he will not marry her to anyone. Just to demolish his pride, the gods make the bridge fall each night."

Rajan was surprised to hear that the tree, the elephant and the king were all suffering because of their own doings. He thanked the holy man for the answers and started his journey home.

First, he went to the king's palace and told him what the sage had said. The king realised his mistake and immediately married his daughter to Rajan. And behold! The bridge that was erected that day did not tumble down at night.

Rajan resumed his journey with his bride and reached the dense *sal* forest. It was nearly afternoon when they reached the spot where the elephant waited.

Rajan went up to the elephant and told him what the holy man had said.

"Why don't you and your bride ride on my back?" asked the elephant.

As soon as Rajan and the princess sat on the elephant's back, his trunk came loose!

"Thank you, son," said the elephant gratefully. "Since you have helped me so unselfishly, I will serve you all my life."

Rajan and the princess now rode the elephant to the mango tree.

The mango tree was glad to see Rajan and his bride. When Rajan told the tree the reason for its withering, the tree offered, "Why don't you dig the pots up from my roots?"

Wanting to help the tree, Rajan took a sturdy stick and started digging. One by one all ten pots were removed from the roots and within seconds the tree stood erect and started flowering.

"Oh! This is a miracle!" cried the mango tree. "Thank you, son. Since you have helped me bloom again, you have earned the pots of gold."

Rajan thanked the mango tree and loaded the pots of gold on the elephant's back and started for his village.

Dusk was falling when Rajan entered his village. Everyone was surprised to see him riding a big elephant. The villagers followed him all the way to his mud house where his mother had lit an oil lamp and was sitting with a plate of *khichdi*, waiting, like every other day, for his return.

The poor old woman was overjoyed to see her son come riding on an elephant with a beautiful princess as his bride and ten pots full of gold coins!

An ancient city in the eastern part of the state of Bihar, Monghyr lies on the banks of the holy river Ganga. The people of the region have always valued the dignity of labour. Travel to far off places for trade and in quest of knowledge and experience was common, both by land and along the river route of the mighty Ganga.

According to the great Indian epic, the *Mahabharata*, in ancient times Monghyr and its adjoining areas were wealthy monarchies. They were famous for their trade, commerce and culture.

Two Birds and a Cooking Pot

Ranjana Goyal

ILLUSTRATED BY
Suddhasattwa Basu

Long ago there lived a farmer called Birju. He was hardworking and honest. He led a very happy life in the village of Lalroo. His wife, Shanti was the best *ghoomar* dancer in the whole village. She would don colourful *ghagras, kurtis* and *odhinis*. She also wore silver anklets on her feet and a big silver *hansli* around her neck. Every day at noon, she would take a pitcher of buttermilk and some *rotis* tied in a cloth to the fields for her husband. She would balance it all on her head and sing as she walked. Her anklets and bangles made sweet, tinkling music all the while.

Once there was no rain. The whole village was in the grip of a drought. The land was parched. Not a blade of grass grew anywhere. Birju spent all his savings and had to sell everything in the house, one by one, to keep the home fires burning. Soon they were literally starving. One night, when the children went to bed, Birju said to his wife, "We cannot go on like this. Tomorrow morning we will go to some other place to find work."

She agreed readily.

The next morning Birju got ready to leave the village with his wife and children. There was nothing left in their house except for a *lota* and a cooking pot. They took these with them.

They walked on and on and grew very tired and hungry. Birju said at last, "Let us rest under the shade of this tree."

His wife Shanti replied, "All right, but what about food?"

"Let's see," he said.

Birju now called for his eldest son Kishana and said, "Son, you go into the nearby forest, bring some grass and twist a rope."

"Yes, *Bapu,*" the boy nodded.

Then he called for his second son and said, "Shamu, go and collect some dry twigs."

"Don't worry, father, I will bring them in a minute," he replied cheerfully, and ran towards some trees nearby.

Shanti thought to herself, "They are trying to find something to cook. In the meantime let me prepare the hearth." She called out to her daughter who was lying in the shade of a tree. "Kammo, my child, help me set up the hearth, so that we are ready to cook whatever your father brings."

Kammo brought three even–looking stones, one by one. The mother cleaned the stones and prepared the hearth. The eldest son made a rope, while the second one brought a big bundle of twigs. Shanti lit the fire and put the pot on the fire.

On that very tree lived a pair of birds, Chakwa and Chakwi. They were observing all the activity with keen interest. They could not understand what the people down below were doing.

Chakwi said to Chakwa, "Look, they have lighted a fire and put their cooking pot on it, but they have nothing to cook. What will they cook? I am terribly afraid."

Chakwa consoled her and said, "Hush! Don't worry. I will go and find out."

Chakwa flew down and said, "Brother, you have nothing to cook. What will you do with this pot?"

Birju was a quick-witted man. He shot back, "We will catch hold of both of you, cook you in this pot and make a good meal of you."

Chakwa became very nervous. He said, "My dear brother, please don't kill us. If you promise not to kill, cook and eat us, I will give you a lot of money."

"All right," Birju replied. "I promise."

Chakwa said, "If you dig three feet under this tree you will find a pitcher of gold coins. You can keep it."

Father and sons dug under the tree and found a pitcher full of gold coins, just as Chakwa had said. They were overjoyed and returned to their village.

Birju was a wise man. With the money he bought land, a pair of bullocks, seeds to sow and a milch cow. In the course of time, he harvested a lush crop of wheat.

His neighbour Bhola and his wife were very jealous when they saw the family prosper. One day, Bhola's wife observed to her husband, "Listen, not long ago they were starving. Where have they got all this wealth from?"

Bhola agreed, "Yes, you are right. It is very strange. I will try to find out."

The next day, when Birju was ploughing his fields, Bhola arrived there and asked him in a very friendly tone, "Birju, you are a wealthy man now. How did all this happen?"

Birju was a very simple person. He told Bhola the whole story of his good fortune. Bhola went home and narrated the story to his wife. He said, "Tomorrow, we will also go to the same place and bring back a lot of wealth."

The next day the two left with their children. By the time they reached the spot, they were all very hungry and tired. They decided to rest, searched for the same tree and sat in its shade.

Bhola called out to his elder son, "Gopal, my son, go to the forest, bring some grass and twist a rope."

But Gopal shot back, "I cannot go. Don't you see my feet are tired after walking for so long?" Saying that he lay down in the shade of the tree.

Bhola called his other son and said, "Ramu, go and collect some dry twigs."

"Oh! Bapu, why don't you tell Gopal? He is just lying under the tree, doing nothing. He is so lazy!" Ramu flatly refused to do anything.

Now the mother called out for her daughter, Sukhia. "Sukhia dear, go and bring three stones so that we can prepare a hearth, light a fire and cook our food."

Sukhia retorted, "Amma, you are always ordering me around to do this and that. I am tired. By the way, what *is* there to cook?" she asked rudely.

Her mother kept quiet.

Bhola got up quietly, brought some grass and made a rope himself. Then he went to collect some twigs. His wife went and brought three stones, lighted a fire and put a pot on the fire.

Sitting up in the tree, Chakwa and Chakwi listened to the family talk and observed the whole scene. The two smiled quietly.

After some time, Chakwi enquired, "Dear, will they catch us, cook and eat us up?"

"Huh, don't be silly!" said Chakwa, smiling. "How can they catch and eat us? Anyhow, I will go and find out."

He flew down and asked, "Oh, brother, you have nothing to cook. What will you cook in this empty pot?"

Bhola replied, "We will catch you with this rope, kill you and cook you both in this pot!"

When Chakwa heard this he laughed heartily, "Ha! Ha! Ha! You cannot catch us. Birju and his family were different. They could have caught us because they understood the wisdom of unity. And we gave them all that wealth to save our lives. But you...? Ha! Ha! Ha! Go back home!"

With that, Chakwa and Chakwi flew away.

This story is from the state of Haryana. Its people are hardworking and fun-loving, and dance and sing when the crop is ready for harvesting. 'Ghoomar' is a popular dance of the region. Most of the folk tales from this area are based on farming and village life.

The Talisman
A STORY FROM BENGAL

SARLA BHATIA

ILLUSTRATED BY
PULAK BISWAS

"Yesterday's barber is today's courtier. Our Maharaja has gone mad!" frowned Beni Parsad Mukhopadhayay. Bitterness and jealousy oozed from every word.

"Don't you know, a barber among men and a crow among birds are both crooks? God save our kingdom!" exclaimed Ganga Parsad Banerjee.

These gentlemen were ministers in the court of Maharaja Krishan Chander, ruler of Bengal three hundred years ago. And the target of their venom was the barber Gopal Bhand, recently appointed a courtier, in appreciation of his humour, wit and intelligence.

Gopal could unravel knotty issues or drive a basic truth home with his simple and good-natured jokes. His rise, from an ordinary villager to a member of the governing council of the state, was so swift that the rich elite and ministers of the court had become his sworn enemies.

Beni Parsad and Ganga Parsad called in the chief of security, Jang Bahadur, to discover the secret of Gopal's success. After a few days he reported, "Sir, Gopal is a devotee of Kali Ma. The goddess has granted him a talisman."

"Now we know the truth!" said Beni Parsad with satisfaction.

"What is our next move?" asked Ganga Parsad.

"To rob him of his talisman and show up his real worth to the king and to all our citizens," replied Beni Parsad.

"I will not rest till I see Gopal Bhand shave a donkey! This cheat will learn his lesson for fooling us all!" added Ganga Parsad. Everyone laughed.

The ministers asked Jang Bahadur to collect two strong men from the city's

best wrestling grounds. The two should be accompanied by two good fighters who knew how to wield their sticks! All four were to raid Gopal's house after dark and force him to part with the talisman. They agreed that they would use Kali Ma's precious gift to become rich and successful together. But each one had a plan of his own, to rob the other two of the talisman in the days to come.

Gopal Bhand lived in a small house on the outskirts of the city. The four strong men and Jang Bahadur broke into the house when the world around was soundless and still. In spite of thousands of stars, the night was very dark.

Gopal Bhand was tied tightly to his bed while he was asleep. And then the men let loose with their sticks and fists. Neither a dog barked nor a cat mewed. Only Gopal Bhand cried out, "Oh, this is killing me! Please stop this madness. Tell me what you want! Money? A favour from the king? I will do whatever you want, but don't beat me!"

Jang Bahadur asked his men to stop and had them light a lantern.

"Give me your talisman. Nothing more – nothing less."

"I have no talisman, my dear sir," pleaded Gopal Bhand.

"You cannot fool me. How else can you explain your winning ways?"

"Come on now, and give me that jewel which the goddess gave you!" Jang Bahadur was even more stern now.

Gopal Bhand had a brainwave. He thought, "These men need to be given a dose of their own medicine." Aloud, he said innocently, "I am sorry that I misled you. You may have the talisman. But it is buried at my farmhouse. You can carry me to that place right away. Are you willing, Jang Bahadur?"

"That's it! Now you are talking sense. Loosen those ropes, boys," commanded the security chief. He asked his captive, "How do we go there?"

"Wait! I am hurt and bruised all over. Please ask one of your men to boil some milk in the kitchen. A pinch of saffron, lying in that small box, should be added. As soon as I have drunk the milk, I shall be ready." Outwardly, Gopal now appeared ready to help them.

Gopal Bhand savoured his hot glass of milk. Then he bade one of the wrestlers apply a poultice of turmeric to his wounds. Now his captors were his captives. He enjoyed his new role.

"Jang Bahadur, I am too heavy to walk. Ask your men to lift me on their shoulders, two at a time. Since there are four of them, each pair can take turns. My farm is only half an hour away. We should be there very soon."

Gopal's words were quite encouraging. Anyway, they had no choice except to give in.

Gopal Bhand was huge and heavy. The men had come with the hope of securing a prize. Now they were forced to carry a big load, known to be a shrewd trickster. Were they being led up the garden path? Perspiring and fatigued, they somehow managed to reach the farmhouse. Their leader had the house opened and settled himself comfortably on a string cot in the verandah.

"Tell us, where have you hidden the talisman?" Jang Bahadur burst out angrily.

"Calm down, please. This farmhouse is not safe from thieves and burglars. Therefore, I have buried the jewel deep in a field. The moon has already come up in the sky and there is moonlight all over the fields. It should be easy for your men to dig out the talisman."

"Now, don't try to be clever. Show us the spot where you have hidden that talisman," growled one of the musclemen.

"Gentlemen, each of you can try his luck. Actually I have forgotten the exact location. But I remember that it was a similar night and I was standing in the field at a position where the moon shone exactly over my head. I kept moving as the moon travelled in the sky. I dug one long deep, furrow across the entire field. It was just the beginning of the day, so I prayed to the Almighty and, with closed

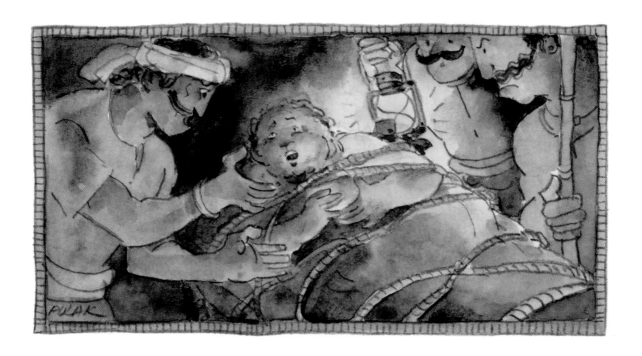

eyes, threw the talisman into the furrow. Then I filled up the furrow with the earth lying around.

"You can do just what I did that night. The four of you can spread yourselves along the field. One is sure to strike luck. Trust me, your hard work will definitely be rewarded." Gopal Bhand directed them to position themselves under the moon.

While the four men began to dig, Gopal sprawled out on the cot and fell into a deep slumber. The entire field was dug up, with a large number of furrows, each quite deep, but the talisman was nowhere to be found! Seething with anger, the men shook Gopal awake.

"You cheat, you liar, get up! Tell us, where is the talisman?"

"Gentlemen, you have found the talisman. Let me tell you that this talisman will bear fruit for everyone. I will put seeds in the field and after four months we can all share the harvest," Gopal Bhand assured them.

Jang Bahadur could not accept this logic. He arrested Gopal Bhand and took him to the court of Maharaja Krishan Chander. Beni Parsad Mukhopadhayay and Ganga Parsad Banerjee were also present. The trio decided to see to it that Gopal Bhand was punished for his trickery.

"Why have you arrested Gopal Bhand?" enquired the Maharaja. "He is an honourable man," he added.

"Forgive me, my Lord," started Jang Bahadur. "This man is nothing but a low cheat. He promised to give me the talisman that grants wealth and happiness. Instead, he led us to his farmhouse and had his field dug up. My men worked there the entire night without finding the talisman!" he concluded angrily.

The Maharaja now asked Gopal Bhand, "Is it true that you promised to give them the talisman? And that you failed to keep your promise?"

"Sire, it is true that I promised I would give them a talisman. Contrary to their allegation, I have fulfilled my promise. I have given a talisman to each of them," was Gopal's prompt reply.

But neither Jang Bahadur nor any of the other men accepted Bhand's assertion. So the Maharaja again asked his courtier to clarify.

"It's very simple, sir. These men do not know their own capabilities. I asked each of them to position himself right under the moon. You can ask them to confirm or deny this," Gopal Bhand stated emphatically.

None of the five refuted his statement, after which Gopal continued, "My Lord, the moon shining on their heads was a clear indication that the brain within the head represents a talisman. I use the talisman, which is my brain, to earn wealth and respect in society and to keep good health. All these help me to be happy. Can they or anyone else, present in this court, deny that God has given us all a talisman? It is for us to make use of this invaluable gift for our own benefit and for that of others."

All those present in court applauded Gopal Bhand's wise words. And to this day, we remember the jester who was wiser than many men living then and now.

'Bhands' are a nomadic tribe known from the Middle Ages for their skill in the performing arts. Moving in small groups, they entertained the common folk, singing and telling humorous stories. The more intelligent from among them became 'court jesters' and at times occupied positions of authority in the government. In this context Birbal was the best known for his wit and wisdom in the court of the Mughal king, the great Akbar. The art of court jesters waned but Gopal Bhand once again revived this position 300 years ago in the provincial court of Bengal and present day Bihar, ruled by Raja Krishan Chander.

The Snake Princess

A STORY FROM ARUNACHAL PRADESH

DIVYA JAIN

ILLUSTRATED BY

VANDANA BIST

Long, long ago, in the Lohit district of Arunachal Pradesh, lived a poor orphan boy called Tara-Oan. He belonged to the Mishmi tribe. He was simple and hard working and lived alone in a small hut near the Lohit River. Every day he went to the river with his nets to catch fish. He then sold the fish in the market and thus earned a living.

But once, for three days, he was not able to catch any fish. There was nothing to eat in his house and he had to sleep hungry.

The next day, weak with hunger, he approached the river and said, "Oh, please God, let me be lucky today!"

Instead of going to his usual place, he walked much further up the river and after saying a small prayer, cast his net into the water. When he pulled out the net, what did he find but a huge black snake with a shiny, spotted body! It was none else but the king of the snakes!

The king of the snakes lived with his family in the waters of the Lohit River. He was now twisting and turning in the net to free himself. But Tara-Oan had a firm grip on the net.

Now the snake king had a daughter named Saila. When she came to know of her father's predicament, she arrived there immediately. Taking human form, she spoke to Tara-Oan. "Please release my father," she requested him. "He is the king of all the snakes and our clan is dependent on him."

"I make a living by selling what I catch from the river," replied Tara-Oan. "I can get a lot of money by selling this snakeskin in the market. If I release him, what will I eat?"

But even as he spoke, Tara-Oan found himself mesmerised by the beauty of the snake princess.

"There is only one condition on which I can spare your father's life," he continued. "You will have to marry me."

The princess was taken aback. She looked shyly at Tara-Oan and said, "Please let me speak to my father."

In snake language, she explained the situation to him. The king was angry at the proposal. "You are a snake princess! How can you marry a mere human being?"

"If I don't marry him, you will never be set free. He is sure to kill you for your skin. Moreover, he appears to be an honourable man. I'm sure everything will work out for the best."

Reluctantly, the king agreed. Saila married Tara-Oan in her human form and they began to live in his village.

Saila soon adjusted to her new life. She would go to the river occasionally to visit her family. When the snake king saw how happy she was, he too was satisfied.

In those days, the chief of the Mishmi tribe was vested with great power. However, he was a cruel and egoistic king. The tribal people were unhappy under his rule, but they dared not go against him.

Tara-Oan, because of his kindness and honesty, was well liked by his tribesmen. The king resented his growing popularity and saw him as a threat.

One day, a few tribesmen approached the king and complained, "Tara-Oan has married an outsider. This goes against our customs. Kindly look into the matter."

The king saw this as a good opportunity to get rid of Tara-Oan.

"You are right," he agreed. "He has married a non-Mishmi girl. He must be punished for this!"

The king could not issue a direct death sentence for such a trivial reason, so he devised an alternate plan. One day he summoned Tara-Oan to his court.

"Tara-Oan!" he said. "Since you have married outside the tribe, the villagers are very unhappy. The matter will be settled by conducting a cockfight in the village square. Your cock will fight mine. If your cock loses, you will have to die."

Tara-Oan was very upset. Since the king had trained fighter cocks, Tara-Oan hardly stood a chance of winning.

Saila saw the dejected face of her husband and asked him what the matter was. She told him not to worry and went quietly to the river. She explained the situation to her father and asked him for help.

The snake king gave her a special cock and asked her to use it during the cockfight. Tara-Oan reached the village square at the appointed time with his cock and the fight began. A number of villagers had gathered to witness the event. There was a lot of excitement as everyone wanted Tara-Oan to win. Amid loud cheers, his cock won the fight.

"Wait!" shouted the king. "The matter is not yet settled. This was just the first condition. The day after tomorrow, there will be a bullfight in the village square. Tara-Oan's bull will fight my royal bull. If his bull loses, he will have to die."

A hush fell over the villagers. The king was being unfair but they dared not speak up. A few of them went to Tara-Oan and offered him their bulls. But he knew it would be of no use. The royal bull was much too strong.

The next day Saila went to the river again and asked her father for help.

The snake king gave a special bull to Saila. Tara-Oan reached the village square with this bull. Many people from the neighbouring villages had gathered to witness the fight.

The two bulls stood facing each other, hot breath blowing from their flared nostrils. With loud bellows they charged at each other and locked their horns in fierce combat. They struggled against each other for quite a while, but finally Tara-Oan's bull won. Everyone clapped and cheered. The tribal king was looking very uncomfortable indeed. Things were not going according to his plan.

"Wait!" he shouted. "The conditions are not yet fulfilled. In two days' time, Tara-Oan has to build a dam on the Lohit River. If he's unable to do so, he'll be beheaded in the same village square where he won the cockfight and the bullfight. He has to build the dam on his own. If any villager tries to help him, he too will be beheaded," announced the king.

Tara-Oan knew that this was an impossible task. For a number of years, the Mishmis and the other tribes had been trying to build a dam on the Lohit River. They had been unable to succeed in this task. How could he do so in two days, and that too unaided?

"Don't worry," Saila comforted him. "We'll find a solution to the problem."

That evening Saila again approached her father for help. This time the snake king gave her a golden basket and explained to her how to use it. The next day Tara-Oan reached the river with the basket. He held it upside down, turned it around thrice and then dipped it in the fast flowing waters of the river. Within minutes, a sturdy dam had sprung up.

The king got a rude shock when he saw the dam. The villagers, however, rejoiced. They lifted Tara-Oan on their shoulders and took him around the

village with much fanfare. Farming was the main occupation of the Mishmis and the dam would solve all their irrigation problems.

The king was enraged. All his plans had failed and Tara-Oan had become a hero. He called everyone and said, "The last condition is yet to be fulfilled. Tomorrow, there will be a wrestling match between Tara-Oan and me. The loser will have to die."

The next day the village square was packed to capacity. News of the duel had spread far and wide. People of the entire Lohit District congregated to witness the fight.

Tara-Oan was strong and healthy but the king was big built and powerful too. Besides, he had been practising the sport for a long time and was an expert at it.

The duel began. Though Tara-Oan was trying his best, it appeared that he would lose.

Saila was holding a large drum in her hands. Suddenly she started beating it loudly. This was a magical drum, which her father had given her. Its rhythm soon had everyone there swaying and dancing to its beat. Not just the people, but the plants, trees and animals too began to dance. Everyone except Tara-Oan was dancing. They danced and danced and danced…It was a wonderful sight indeed!

After a long time, Saila stopped playing the drum. Everyone stopped dancing and fell down, exhausted after the vigorous activity.

Tara-Oan seized the opportunity. He grappled with the tribal king and defeated and killed him.

The Mishmis crowned him king unanimously. Tara-Oan thanked the snake king for his help. Saila became the queen and both ruled successfully for a number of years.

Ever since then, snakes are considered auspicious by the Mishmis.

Situated amid the eastern Himalayas, Arunachal Pradesh is the largest state in northeast India. The various types of forests here provide shelter to different kinds of fauna. Pythons and snakes are commonly found in the lush forests of its temperate zone.

There are about twenty main tribal strains among the people of this state. They are mainly the Mishmis, Khamtis and Singphos. Each tribe has a distinct linguistic, ethical, cultural and social entity, which sets it apart from the others. Members of some of these tribes revere snakes and consider it auspicious if they spot one anywhere.

Gifts for the Worthy

A STORY FROM UTTAR PRADESH

Madhulika Agarwal

ILLUSTRATED BY
Viky Arya

Once upon a time, the ruler of a kingdom of Awadh was holding court when the arrival of a holy man was announced.

The king stood up to greet him with folded hands. "Welcome, saintly one!" he said, bowing.

The bearded sage held up his right hand in blessing. "God bless this kingdom!" he proclaimed. He was dressed in saffron robes, and held a brass vessel in his hand for the offerings people might make to him. A saffron bag hung on his shoulder.

"I have travelled all over the country," he continued, "and I am indeed pleased to observe your kingdom. The people of a village in particular really impressed me – the one that lies close to your capital. They are very hardworking, humble and honest. They toil through the day and enjoy their leisure time together in the evening."

"I am honoured to hear this," the king bowed. Pride was written all over his face.

"I wish to reward the people of this village with some gifts. Come with me to the village square," the holy man commanded, hurrying out.

The king followed him. The ministers and the courtiers followed the king and soon a large group of people was behind them.

When he reached the village square, the sage climbed on to the raised platform built around a big banyan tree. He put his brass vessel down, then searched in his bag and took out a sparkling white marble.

The people watched him, wondering what he was doing.

"God bless this kingdom!" the holy man cried. He threw the marble down on the ground.

To their astonishment, it turned into a spotless white cow, as white as milk itself. The people had barely stopped exclaiming when he took out a brown marble and flung that down too. It changed into a *maina* bird. Finally, he took out a multi-coloured marble. As the people watched with bated breath, it was transformed into a large doll, the size of a twelve-year old girl.

"Now, listen all of you. This is a wish-fulfilling cow. Her name is Gauri," the holy man patted the cow on her back. "She will appear every morning and provide enough milk for the whole village."

"The whole village!" the people exclaimed, astounded.

He then held the bird in his right hand and stroked her with the left. "This bird, her name is Kajri. She will come and sing for you every afternoon when you all lie down to rest."

"And this doll," he put his hand on the doll's head, "her name is Mohini. She will emerge at night to enthral you with her dancing when you want to relax after a hard day's labour."

The village folk gazed at their gifts wide-eyed. They did not know what to say. They were utterly dumbfounded.

"How can I thank you, holy one!" the king said, overwhelmed at this bounty.

"God bless this kingdom!" proclaimed the sage again. He walked away with a smile.

The villagers danced with joy and celebrated these gifts for two whole days.

Every morning, before the sun rose, Gauri would come and stand under the banyan tree. The villagers would milk her to their heart's content.

Every afternoon, when the sun was moving towards the west, Kajri would alight on the banyan tree. She would sing in such a melodious tone that the whole village would fall asleep in no time.

And every night, when the people had finished their meals and were ready to relax, it was time for Mohini to come and dance, dressed in a gorgeous magenta and green *lehnga-chunri*.

Life seemed perfect in the village. The villagers were happy and so was the king.

But gradually, things began to change. And one day, a dreadful thing happened.

The inhabitants of the village rose at their usual hour and rushed to milk Gauri. But Gauri stood still. She made strange sounds and refused to yield any milk.

The people were shocked and dismayed and went home empty-handed.

In the afternoon they waited for Kajri to come and lull them to sleep as usual. Kajri arrived. But today, she refused to sing. She only made harsh sounds, "*Kaa, kaa, kaa...*"

The villagers were even more disturbed. They lay down for their afternoon naps but could only toss about restlessly.

Then night fell and all of them waited for Mohini in eager anticipation. Mohini arrived at the usual hour. But she too would not dance today.

"No, no, no..." she murmured, in response to their entreaties.

The villagers were almost in tears now.

The same thing happened the next day, and the next.

When the news reached the king, he was equally perturbed. He sent his men around, to all the neighbouring villages, to announce that whoever could decipher what Gauri, Kajri and Mohini were trying to say, would be rewarded handsomely. People came from far and wide, but none could solve the riddle. As for the villagers, they abandoned their work and sat down to bewail their misfortune.

The king was very upset to see his people so unhappy. He sent his men to look for the sage. But he was nowhere to be found.

Life seemed to come to a standstill in the village, and everyone was beginning to give up all hope.

Then one day, Amma, a very old and lame woman, came and sat in front of the banyan tree. "Listen, all of you!" she called out. "Come and listen to me. I can tell you what Gauri, Kajri and Mohini are trying to say."

People mocked her, saying, "The wisest and most learned of men came from far and wide and they could not tell us anything. And you, an ignorant old woman who spends the day selling garlands outside the temple, claim you can! What can *you* do?"

"Just let me try. Call everyone here," the old woman smiled knowingly.

"We will not! You have come to make a fool of us," the elders of the village declared.

"It's all right if you do not believe me," said the old woman. "I'll just go back to the temple."

"Go, then. *Go!*" Everyone shouted together.

The old woman was about to leave when the king's chariot happened to pass that way. He ordered his charioteer to stop and asked what the commotion was all about.

When he heard the whole story, he commanded, "Let her try."

The village folk had to agree.

Early the next morning, when Gauri made strange sounds, Amma listened to her intently. In the afternoon, she heard Kajri's call, and at night she gave diligent ear to Mohini.

Then she said she would proclaim her observations the next morning, in front of the king and the whole village. The priest went to the king's court to request him to come to the village square for the old woman's announcement.

Early the next morning, when everyone had gathered, Amma began. She bowed to the king and said, "Your Majesty! Gauri is repeatedly saying, 'Intolerable! Intolerable!'"

"Intolerable! What is intolerable?" the king enquired.

"She is very sad at the state of affairs in this village. People fight every morning to get the milk first. Also, since it is free, they try to take more than they need and then they stuff themselves with milk and sweets made from it."

"Oh, ho!" the king remarked.

"Her milk will not flow for people who fight over it," she added.

"And what about Kajri?" the king asked.

"Unbearable, unbearable!' This is what she keeps repeating."

"Now, what is unbearable for her?" the king asked.

"She cannot sing here any more. When she came to this village, the people were very hardworking and her job was to soothe them for a while. But now, it seems that she has made them lazy. In the afternoons, they sleep over her song and will not get up for hours on end. She will not sing for such lazy people."

"Oh...!" The king was beginning to understand the situation.

"And what about Mohini?" the king asked.

"Unbelievable, unbelievable!'" Amma laughed.

"And what is unbelievable now?" The king grew very anxious.

"It is unbelievable that these village folk have become so rude and foul-tongued. Earlier they were polite and humble. But now they fight and abuse the people from neighbouring villages who come to see her dance. They don't let them in."

"But why?" The king was bewildered.

"They claim that Mohini is theirs alone," Amma laughed.

"Is that so?" remarked the king. The puzzle had been solved. But two questions were still lingering in his mind.

He said, "Amma, how did you interpret their language?"

"It was very simple. Seeing how the villagers were behaving, I guessed it even before Gauri, Kajri and Mohini started acting this way!"

"Then why didn't you tell us all this while?" the king was puzzled.

"Things are better told at the right time," Amma replied, and began to walk away.

"Wait! What reward do you want?" the king asked.

"Ah! The grand reward! All I want is that our folk become their old selves again," Amma replied. And this time she did not wait for a response. She just walked away.

True to Amma's wish, the villagers became their old, simple, hardworking selves again and to everybody's great relief Gauri, Kajri and Mohini also went back to normal.

Situated in the north on the fertile Gangetic plain, Uttar Pradesh is the most densely populated state in India. It shares a border with Nepal and several other Indian states. It is watered by the rivers Ganga, Jamuna, Gomati and Ghaghra and is one of the largest producers of food grains and sugar cane. Awadh, located in central Uttar Pradesh, is a region with great religious and cultural significance. It is the home of the *Ramayana* and the birthplace of Lord Rama, Ayodhya, is located here. In later times, the Nawabs of Awadh developed a unique culture in the fields of music and literature.

This story is an ethical tale, and cannot be considered very region specific.

A Matter of Honour

A STORY FROM RAJASTHAN

PRATIBHA NATH

ILLUSTRATED BY

NEETA GANGOPADHYA

There once lived a man named Ranbir Singh. He was a *thakur* by birth, a member of the warrior Rajput race. Ranbir Singh stood over six feet tall and had limbs to match that magnificent height. Set in a bronzed face, his eyes sparkled with vigour and well-being. But the pride of his life was his moustache. Coal black and bristling, it stood for a vigorous, hot-blooded man who would readily lay down his life to protect his honour.

Ranbir Singh lived in old-time Rajputana. He was a rich man. On lands inherited from his forefathers, he raised millets and mustard and reared camels. Business was good and every second year saw a room added to Ranbir Singh's mansion.

But the good times did not last. Ranbir Singh was as generous as he was proud and generosity often clouded his better judgement. He also liked to live in style, dress in style, entertain lavishly and ply his family with expensive gifts. Since there was enough money flowing in, he even grew a little indifferent towards his business.

As luck would have it, there followed a period of drought and Ranbir Singh's fortunes slowly took a turn for the worse. For three successive years, his crops withered on the stalk and a mysterious disease hit his camels, killing many of them. And before long, in Ranbir Singh's house, money became scarce.

Ranbir Singh had a large family and several old retainers. His pride would not allow him to cut down on expenses. To keep up the old standard of living, he began to sell his belongings one by one. When these were gone, he mortgaged, his lands and then his house, to raise money. But in time, even that money was spent and Ranbir Singh realised that for sheer survival, he would have to go to a local moneylender to seek yet another loan.

The moneylender took one look at him and immediately sensed that something was wrong, for Ranbir Singh looked subdued. He stood quietly, on one side, as if trying to avoid the moneylender's eye.

But the moneylender was a good man at heart. He did not like to see the *thakur* so disturbed. When the customary greetings had been exchanged, he said warmly, "Please step in, *Thakur sa*. Take a seat. Is there anything I can do for you?"

Ranbir Singh entered with heavy steps and sat down. It was some time before he spoke and when he did, the sound seemed to come from far away. It was not the full-throated, booming voice of the *thakur* that people knew.

"*Seth sa*," he said slowly, "as you know, fortune does not smile on anyone for ever..."

"True, true," said the moneylender, in genuine agreement. "I have seen the rich fall from the height of their glory when they least expected it. But what makes you talk in that manner?"

Ranbir Singh took a deep breath. "*Seth sa*," he said, "I talk in this manner because this is just what has happened in my case, too." He might have said something more, but the moneylender stopped him, for the *thakur's* voice was quavering, ever so slightly.

"*Thakur sa*," said the moneylender heartily, "my people have known yours for generations. The relationship between our two families was not born yesterday. I can see that you are disturbed about something. Come, come, you can trust me. Just tell me what you wish and it shall be done, as soon as possible. What is more, nobody except the two of us will ever know about it."

Ranbir Singh looked at the moneylender gratefully. But he was only too well aware of the ways of moneylenders. He knew that he would not part with a single *cowrie* without adequate security. And what could he, *Thakur* Ranbir Singh, a landowner merely in name, offer by way of security? He had nothing left, absolutely nothing.

All this time the moneylender was looking at him intently, searching his face for an answer. At last Ranbir Singh found his voice and said, haltingly, "*Seth sa*, I need a loan of a thousand rupees. But I have nothing left to offer by way of

security. All the jewellery, all the silver and other valuables that I possessed are gone. Even the house is mortgaged. I can only offer you my word of honour that I shall repay the loan…Now my fate is in your hands, *Seth sa*. You alone can save me and my family."

It took a great effort for a proud man like Ranbir Singh to utter these words and to admit that only the moneylender stood between him and utter ruin. His face was drained of all colour. Meanwhile, the moneylender had ordered a glass of ice sherbet to be placed before him.

"Take a sip, *Thakur sa*," he coaxed. "You will feel better."

As Ranbir Singh raised a shaky hand towards the glass, the moneylender leaned back against his bolster, deep in thought. He really was in a fix.

Never in his life had he loaned out money without security. Neither had his father or grandfather or any other ancestor that he knew of. It was totally against business principles. It…it simply wasn't done…At the same time he could see that Ranbir Singh was in deep trouble and he wished to help an old family friend.

"*Thakur sa*," said the moneylender, "I trust you completely. I have no doubt whatsoever that you will, in the course of time, repay the loan. But is there nothing, nothing at all that you can offer by way of security right now? I…I am faced with a real problem. I must make an entry in my ledger and you must sign it. But no deal of this kind is valid unless I also put down the words, 'Against adequate security'. Take your time, sit comfortably and think it over. The money is waiting for you…"

The moneylender had tried to soften the blow all right. Ranbir Singh covered his face with both hands and sank back into silence.

As he sat in the shop, the *thakur* was a deeply frustrated man. His hopes had taken a beating and for a while it seemed that all was over. But suddenly Ranbir Singh realised that his pride was still alive and, with it, his sense of family honour. He could not give up! Through the haze of disappointment surrounding him, he began to re-live the days of his childhood and youth. Maybe somewhere he would find the glimmer of an answer to his problem…

In his mind's eye Ranbir Singh saw the majestic figure of his grandfather. All of six feet tall and so erect, wearing his turban with such grace. A little tickle of joy stirred within Ranbir Singh, for didn't they all say he had taken after his grandfather – the same height, the same proud mien…? His father, ah yes, his father was shorter by an inch and had never stopped regretting the fact. But he was a fine figure of a man too, with piercing black eyes and a forehead that belonged to nobility, no less.

Ranbir Singh's mind wandered through the maze of old family bonds. His father and grandfather had been very close. They often rode together, young Ranbir Singh riding with either one or the other. His grandfather loved to live in style. And yes, he was rather proud of his appearance too. In particular he was proud of his moustache. Coal black and stiffly pointed, for its owner it was the ultimate symbol of honour and dignity, as it was for his grandson. Ranbir Singh recalled a story that he had heard within the family.

Once, his grandfather, Kehar Singh, had gone wild boar hunting with the ruler of a small state. Both men were in their early twenties. But while Kehar Singh was already known to be an excellent shot, the raja was still learning. He told Kehar Singh, "Take your gun along but don't use it except in an emergency. This is my chance to bag my first wild boar. Promise?"

Kehar Singh promised. But the raja was a bit doubtful. He said, "Are you sure you won't forget your promise?"

Thereupon Kehar Singh drew himself up to his full height and roared, "If I do, I promise to cut off my moustache! And you know, Raja *sa*, what cutting off a moustache means to a *thakur* – the ultimate mark of dishonour."

This had silenced the raja, Ranbir Singh had heard, who even apologised for doubting the *thakur's* word.

Ranbir Singh's hand reached up to his own moustache and suddenly a thought flashed through his mind, a thought which brought a flicker of hope. Turning to the moneylender, he exclaimed, "*Seth sa*, I do have something that can stand security against a loan. My moustache. You know what each hair of it means to a *thakur*. Here, this is my security!"

With these words, Ranbir Singh plucked a hair from his moustache, placed it on his palm and offered it ceremoniously to the moneylender. "This hair is more valuable to me than all the money I ever had," he declared.

The moneylender was dumbfounded. For a moment he simply stared at the hair, while a frown creased his brow. Then he looked at the *thakur's* face and realised that it had begun to glow again with something akin to pride. It was like the dawn of a new day...

The frown disappeared from the moneylender's face. He smiled, picked up the hair, placed it in a small silver casket and locked the casket up inside his safe.

"I accept your security, *Thakur sa*," he announced, adding emphatically, "I know you will pay back the money so you can recover that hair from your moustache and your honour is not tarnished."

At a sign from him, his clerk brought a cloth bag jingling with a thousand silver rupees. Ranbir Singh signed the ledger happily, thanked the moneylender and walked back home with the money.

This story comes from the state of Rajasthan, (old-time Rajputana) which lies along the western border of India. It is an arid region, but with a rich and colourful history and folklore. For hundreds of years, this region was dotted with big and small independent states, each ruled by a raja. These states have now been combined to form one. The people of Rajasthan are known to be fearless and self-respecting. To them personal honour means everything and they will not allow it to be blemished.

GLOSSARY

alpana	-	A kind of *rangoli* (a design painted on the floor with rice paste) special to Bengal, made on all festive occasions.
amma	-	Mother.
bapu	-	Father.
bonga	-	Spirit.
charpai	-	Light bed.
cowrie	-	A small unit of money used in earlier times.
dal	-	Lentils.
datun	-	A soft twig of the *neem* or margosa tree, used to clean teeth.
devas	-	Gods.
dhol	-	Drum.
gamucha	-	A kind of cloth with a special weave, a symbol of love and respect.
ghaghra	-	Long, gathered skirt worn with a blouse and veil.
ghee	-	Clarified butter.
ghoomar	-	A type of folk dance.
gitta	-	Anklebone.
hansli	-	Choker.
hukkah	-	Indian pipe.
jalebi	-	Indian sweet.
jawar	-	Millets.
jhanjhar	-	Anklet.
khichdi	-	A dish of rice and lentils cooked together with salt, water and spices.
kshatriya	-	The warrior caste.
kurti	-	Blouse worn with ghaghra.
laddoo	-	Round Indian sweet.
lathi	-	Heavy stick.
lehnga chunri	-	Long gathered skirt and veil worn by women.
Lord Indra	-	The rain god.
lota	-	A kind of metal vessel.
mahua	-	The tree *Bassia latifolia* and its flower from which an intoxicating drink is made.
maina	-	A kind of singing bird, brown in colour.
mekhla-chaddar	-	A two-piece Assamese dress for women consisting of two long strips of cloth— *mekhla*, the lower portion worn like a long skirt, *chadar*, the upper portion, a cloth draped over the chest and shoulders.
neem	-	Margosa, a tree with medicinal properties.
odhni	-	Veil.
pithe	-	A special sweet made with rice flour, coconut, jaggery and milk.
pous parvan	-	A winter festival of Bengal held on Makar Sankranti (mid-January) when the goddess Lakshmi is worshipped.
puran poli	-	A Maharashtrian sweet.
rangoli	-	Design painted on floor with coloured rice paste.
roti	-	Round flat, unleavened bread.
sa	-	A term of respect.
sal	-	The tree *Shorea robusta*, commonly used for timber.
sadhu	-	Holy man, ascetic.
sahib	-	Sir.
seth	-	Moneylender, rich businessman.
thakur	-	A *kshatriya*, member of the warrior caste; also used as a term of address.
vaid	-	Traditional physician specialising in Indian herbal medicine.
veena	-	A stringed musical instrument.

ABOUT OUR AUTHORS

Girija Rani Asthana writes for children of all age groups, especially for pre-primary and primary classes. She has written several picture books, short stories, biographies - both in Hindi and English and won many awards. At present, she is Vice-President of the Association of Writers and Illustrators for Children and looks after their exhibitions.

Swapna Dutta has been writing for children for nearly three decades and has over thirty-five titles to her credit, including translations. She has received many awards for her work, among them a national fellowship. She also writes for adults and has been published by nearly all the national newspapers, journals and periodicals abroad.

Mamata Pandya is an environmental educator involved in developing innovative and creative teaching-learning material for educators and children. She has over forty publications (as author, co-author and editor). She lives in Ahmedabad, Gujarat.

Nilima Sinha has won several national level awards for her books for children, which include popular mystery and adventure novels, historical fiction, short stories, picture books, biographies and plays. She writes in Hindi and English. At present she is the President, AWIC and Vice-President, IBBY.

Deepa Agarwal has written more than thirty books in English and Hindi and contributes regularly to leading periodicals in India and abroad. Along with many others, she has received the National Award for Children's Literature for her picture book, *Ashok's New Friends* and two fellowships for researching children's literature. She also writes fiction and poetry for adults, and translates from Hindi into English.

Thangam Krishnan has been writing for children for a long time. Her short stories, folk tales and historical fiction have won her many awards. She has also written research-based articles on children's literature.

Devika Rangachari is currently doing her PhD from the Department of History, University of Delhi. She has been writing for children since 1994 and has written several award-winning novels and short stories. Her book, *Growing Up*, was nominated for the Honour List of the International Board on Books for Young People (IBBY) in 2002. Her interests are reading and writing.

Nita Berry writes short stories, picture and activity books, historical biographies and full length non-fiction for children of all ages. She has won several awards for her work including the Shankar's Medal for *The Story of Time*. She is presently Secretary of AWIC and on the editorial board of its quarterly journal, *Writer and Illustrator*. She has represented India in several international seminars and workshops.

Kamlesh Mohindra has to her credit mystery stories, folk tales, picture and activity books in English and Hindi. Many have won awards. She is particularly sought after for creating child-friendly textbooks for schools.

Surekha Panandiker is a well-established author of children's books. She writes both in English and Marathi. She has over forty books to her credit and is an eloquent storyteller. She has represented India in both national and international seminars on children's literature and storytelling. Currently, she is the convener of the AWIC Library Project.

Indira Ananthakrishnan writes with passion to inspire and entertain young minds. Writing short stories is a direct, brief and delightful way to reach children, she feels. She has had many stories published, on a variety of universal themes.

Dipavali Debroy teaches Economics and writes freelance for children and on Indian mythology, in English and Bengali. She lives and works in Delhi, but spent her childhood in Bengal. *Kusum* and *The Mystery of the Ancient Platter* are among her published novels for children.

Amrita Bogra is a freelance writer who writes features and short stories for newspapers, magazines and books. She is also a keen social worker.

Mira Garg spent her early years in a tea-estate in Upper Assam where the beauty, peace and quiet inspired her creative mind. She has written poetry and prose from childhood. She is confident that creative people like writers and artists will inspire and keep alive the wonderful world of books for young and old.

Vinita Krishna has been writing for the younger age group for the last twenty years. She has pioneered the publication of adapted literatures in India for children with special needs (disabled children). Her special tactile sensory books have won international acclaim.

Vijaylakshmi Nagaraj has been an educationist for over two decades. Her special focus has been on integrating storytelling with textbook learning. She is also involved in storytelling for sick children in hospitals using her own handmade puppets. She has written research-oriented articles on children's literature and is the author of the series *Anytime Stories*.

Bilkiz Alladin writes adventure stories, plays and poems for children. She is also a researcher and has written historical plays and ballets. She has received several awards for her work, including the Chevalier of Arts and Letters from the French Government and an honorary doctorate from the University of Louisiana, USA.

Santhini Govindan has written more than twenty books for children including non-fiction, poetry, picture books and short stories, and more than seventy-five of her articles have been published in leading national dailies and magazines in India and abroad. She has won many prizes for her work, and has been awarded two National Fellowships for Literature from the Department of Culture, Government of India, for projects connected with children's literature in India.

Somya Dave works for the government and enjoys writing for children, particularly for her young son. Her short stories have been published in children's magazines and as part of various collections.

Dr Varsha Das, writer, poet and translator has been writing for children for the past forty-two years in Gujarati, Hindi and English. Her books for children have been published by reputed publishers including UNICEF.

Paulomi Misra is a computer software expert who writes for children. She has over fifteen non-fiction books to her credit, apart from creative work in fantasy and mystery writing for magazines and newspapers.

Ranjana Goyal has a strong teaching background. She is a voracious reader of books and is interested in literature for children and writes for them. She is also involved in social work.

Sarla Bhatia began life as a freelance journalist thirty-five years ago and has contributed to several leading magazines. She writes articles of general interest, short stories and books which include collections of poems. Many have won awards.

Divya Jain writes for children in Hindi and English. Her stories and book reviews have been published in various magazines and journals. She has written a book for Scholastic India. She also writes scripts for radio programmes.

Madhulika Agarwal has written many short stories for children. She has two published books to her credit, besides contributions in magazines. She is on the editorial board of *Writer and Illustrator*, the quarterly journal published by the Association of Writers and Illustrators for Children.

Pratibha Nath is a storyteller, journalist and one-time teacher of English. She writes because she enjoys it. Her work has received several literary awards.

ABOUT OUR ILLUSTRATORS

Viky Arya obtained her Masters in Fine Arts from Banaras Hindu University. She has conceptualised and developed many national and multimedia campaigns on child-related subjects, some of which have received national and international awards. She has illustrated several books for children. In 2002 she received the NCERT National Award for illustration.

Suddhasattwa Basu is a painter, illustrator and animation film-maker. He studied at the College of Art, Calcutta. One of the foremost illustrators of children's books in India, among the books he has illustrated and designed are Khushwant Singh's *Nature Watch*, Ruskin Bond's *To Live in Magic* and V. Sulaiman's *The Homecoming*.

Pulak Biswas is a pioneering illustrator and painter, who has been associated with all the leading publishing houses for children in India. He has also worked for publishers in the United States, Austria and Germany. He was awarded the Grand Honorary Diploma in the Biennale of Illustrations, Bratislava, in 1967. He received the prestigious BIB Plaque (Bratislava) in 1999 for his book, *Tiger on a Tree*.

Sujasha Dasgupta is a graduate of the College of Art, Delhi. She has worked as a freelance illustrator for the last sixteen years with leading publishing houses and magazines in India, like Katha, Children's Book Trust, National Book Trust, Ratna Sagar, Scholastic India, and the popular children's magazine, *Children's World*.

Neeta Gangopadhya is a graduate of the College of Art, Delhi and has illustrated several books for Children's Book Trust, National Book Trust, Ratna Sagar, Frank Brothers, Scholastic India and Macmillan India. She participated in the Biennale of Illustrations, Bratislava in 1995.

Taposhi Ghoshal studied at the College of Art, Delhi and began freelancing in 1993. She has illustrated and designed several children's books, magazines and textbooks. She received the Kalatrayee Award from the Directorate of Education in 1985. Her work has been exhibited in India and abroad.

Tapas Guha did his post-graduation in Commerce from Delhi. He has been illustrating for children for over a decade and has worked with leading publishing houses and children's magazines in India.

Jagdish Joshi has illustrated more than 150 books and won many awards, including the prestigious Noma Concours in 1983 for his picture-book, *One Day* (1983). He was nominated from India for the 1998 Hans Christian Andersen Award for illustration.

Atanu Roy is an illustrator, artist, cartoonist and designer. He has illustrated more than hundred books for children and won the Children's Choice Award for book illustrations in 1989. He has won awards at the 1983, 1984, and 1986 Yomiuri Shimbun International Cartoon Contests and contributed to Bob Geldof's *Caroonaid*, released at the Seoul Olympics. He has worked as an independent art designer in Tokyo and subsequently as a freelance designer and artist. He has his own design studio, ArtGym.

Subir Roy graduated in Applied Art from the Government College of Art, Calcutta. He got a Special Jury mention in BIB, Bratislava for his illustrations in the picture book, *The Woman and the Crow*. He has contributed to the children's magazines *Cricket* and *Cicada* published in the United States. Subir Roy is presently Art Executive with the Children's Book Trust.

Sujata Singh did a three-year Diploma in Graphic Design and Illustration at Wimbeldon School of Art and Design, London. She has worked as a designer and illustrator for *Target*, *India Today*, *Business Today*, *Cosmopolitan*, *Teens Today*, *Namaste*, Penguin Books India, Katha, Ratna Sagar, and Kali for Women, among others. She has had several exhibitions of her work in India and abroad.

Sonali Biswas did her B.F.A. in Art History from Kala Bhavan, Vishwa Bharati University, Shantiniketan in 1996 and M.A. in the same subject from M.S University, Baroda in 1998. She has been a part-time lecturer in Art History in Delhi College of Art. Presently she is working as a freelance illustrator and has worked for publishers such as Puffin and Rupa & Co. She received the 2000 Noma Concours Runners-up Award for Children's Book Illustration from Japan and Honourable Mention Award in BAIJ 2002 (Biennale of Asian Illustrators Japan).

Vandana Bist graduated from the College of Art, New Delhi in 1986. She has specialised in children's book illustration and writing. Vandana received the Noma Concours consolation prize from Japan in 1988 and has also been awarded for a short story by Children's Book Trust as well as by Katha. A free-lancer, she has illustrated books for leading publishers like Puffin and Rupa & Co. among others and has had several short stories published. She also has experience in theatre.